Stay bold!

AMONG THE
CRIMSON SNOW

ANGELA R. WATTS

Copyright 2024 © Angela R. Watts. All rights reserved.

https://angelarwatts.com/

Cover design by Tyrone "SycrosD4" Barnes. All rights reserved.

Cover typography by Miblart. All rights reserved.

This book or any portion thereof may not be reproduced or used in any form whatsoever without the written permission of the publisher except the brief use of quotations in a book review.

This is a work of fiction. All names, characters, locations, places, incidents, and so forth are either the product of the author's imagination or used in a fictitious manner. Any similarities to people, living or dead, and actual events, are entirely coincidental.

Printed in the United States of America.

ISBN: 9798328837828

CONTENTS

Dedication	VII
	X
1. PART I	1
2. ONE	1
3. TWO	1
4. THREE	1
5. FOUR	1
6. FIVE	1
7. SIX	1
8. SEVEN	1
9. PART II	1
10. ONE	1
11. TWO	1

12. THREE 1

13. FOUR 1

14. FIVE 1

15. SIX 1

16. SEVEN 1

17. EIGHT 1

18. NINE 1

19. TEN 1

20. ELEVEN 1

21. TWELVE 1

22. THIRTEEN 1

23. FOURTEEN 1

24. FIFTEEN 1

25. SIXTEEN 1

26. SEVENTEEN 1

27. EIGHTEEN 1

28. NINETEEN 1

29. TWENTY 1

30. TWENTY-ONE 1

31. TWENTY-TWO 1
32. PART III 1
33. ONE 1
34. TWO 1
35. THREE 1
36. FOUR 1
37. FIVE 1
38. SIX 1
39. SEVEN 1
40. EIGHT 1
41. PART IV 1
42. ONE 1
43. TWO 1
44. THREE 1
45. FOUR 1
46. SIX 1
47. PART V 1
48. ONE 1
49. TWO 1

50. THREE 1

Author's Note 1

Thank You 1

Music Playlist 1

Also By 1

Author Bio 1

DEDICATION

To the warrior,

with the weary heart

and bloody hands

and empty eyes,

Do not let your spirit wane,

Do not forget the light,

And remember that you are not alone,

you are not forsaken,

And you are not too broken to be loved.

Seek the Light,

Seek love,

Seek goodness,

And when you find these things,

Reveal them to the warriors that stumbles across your path.

With love,

Maude

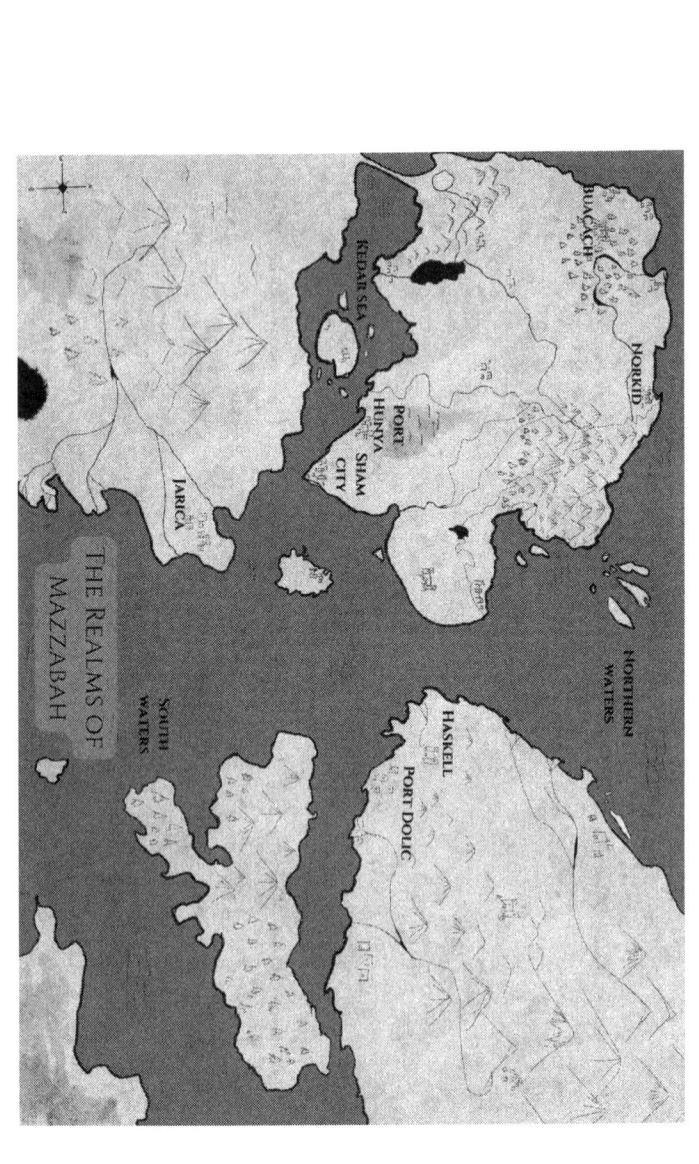

PART I

ONE

There are many good reasons as to why I, a northern priest, was wandering along a highway wearing the clothes I was born in — that is to say, none. And the men and women that passed me on the dirt road, their eyes downcast in shame and cheeks red with dismay, surely thought I was a drunkard, wandering aimlessly along until I fell in a ditch and died, which would be a well-deserved fate.

However, the passerbyers would be wrong in that assumption, and I had more important matters to tend to than to defend my circumstances.

So I called out in the crisp autumn morning, "Good day!" I was not accustomed to what proper greetings should sound like coming from a naked man, so I chose my usual greeting, to be safe. "Have you heard the word of Creator?"

The man in the wagon that bounced slowly along the rocky trail gave me a small glance, huffing, as if I'd asked him for a thousand coins. "Quite rich, coming from the likes of you, Mister!"

"I'm a priest," I said, "though it does not look it. I'll dare say, did Creator's son not hang on the thorned tree naked for our sins? I like to think I'm in good, humble company in my current predicament." I flashed a grin.

"I don't have any money or clothes to offer you." The man whistled, urging his two ponies to go faster on the road.

"I ask for nothing but some thought-provoking company!" I called, still keeping up with the wagon. My long stride was good for much.

The man spat a large mouthful of tobacco onto the road in front of me. It narrowly missed my feet, but I stepped over it and continued on. "I have no need for your god," he said simply, "I have my own gods."

"I came from the north, and we had many gods as well. But there is no one as merciful as Creator." I beamed.

The man laughed hard, looking down at me over the wagon's side. "If your god is so merciful, why are you naked on the highway without a penny to your name?"

"Who needs material possessions?" I asked. "Nothing will accompany me to Creator but my soul."

The man whistled. "I misjudged you for a drunk. I see now that you're a madman." As he ushered the wagon on faster, I slowed slightly, letting them disappear over the hill.

I continued on at a slower pace. I could have gone faster, but the beating I had received made that difficult. But, mercifully, I had no broken bones, and my bruises and gashes would heal.

Probably.

I was a priest, but I was also a man of medicine, and unfortunately, I didn't have anything with me in which to patch my wounds, and I had foraged in the woods early that morning when I woke in the ditch, but had found nothing usable for a remedy.

I walked with a limp and tried to keep my wits about me. I hadn't lost all that much, really: my clothes, a pack of necessities, and what little coin I earned doing small jobs for farmers and the like. I would earn it all back if I reached a village. That was, if any village allowed a madman into their midst.

And unfortunately, I was not in the understanding lands, or in my homeland. I was in the east, where people were quicker to stab you dead than offer you a place beside the fireside.

That was all right. I knew where Creator had called me to come, and it was the east, and to the east I had gone. I'd only been wandering here for two days before I was attacked and mugged, but Creator had not yet informed me why I was in the east, so the east I would stay.

But I was not sure how much ministering I could do in the shape I was in, but I could not ask for charity, and could not earn a job without clothes...

Sighing, I ran a hand over my face. This was a foreign land, and I wasn't sure how to traverse it from here. Still, I could not let my soul be troubled, and I would have to continue on, without doubt.

By nightfall, I saw smoke on the horizon, and I stumbled along the foothills toward civilization.

Just as the sun began to set, a group of men clad in black came down the road, and approached me.

Now, I knew Creator was with me, and knew the number of my days. So, like a fool, I called, "Hallo!"

No sooner had the words left my mouth than the group of men drew bows and arrows, and a few arrows were loosed toward me. One whizzed by my ear, and I froze in my tracks. I had, of course, been in a similar situation, but I had been able to talk my way out of almost every situation before. I would try it again.

"I'm not here to—"

My words fell on deaf ears, and more arrows pierced the heavy dusk. None of them struck me — and I knew the men were merely warning me, and if they wanted me dead, they had a clean shot to do so. I was running out of warning arrows.

I took a step back, but one arrow struck my arm, and then a great yell pierced the air — whose, I was not sure, but it almost sounded like a wild animal of some kind. A large cat, perhaps?

Whatever beast had roared from the woods, it was enough to scare the warriors that approached me.

The men turned and fled.

TWO

Blood ran down my arm from where the arrow had nicked me deeply, but I looked toward the woods.

No wild animal lurched from the dense trees to pounce me and devour me.

Instead, I saw something move in the bushes. Something lean. Tall.

Something almost human.

"Wait!" I ran forward. After all, be it man or beast, did I have anything left to lose but my life, and even that, I did not fear, because I knew where my foolish soul would go.

I staggered into the woods — my quick stride, again, worked wonders. But before I could stop myself, I crashed into something — or *someone*.

Because where the bushes and dense trees ended, a small ravine began.

I fell hard, rolling and toppling like a rock traveling down a waterfall. My landing, however, was much softer, and I hit the ground with a *thud*.

In the dark, I didn't see much, but a grunt came from below me.

"Get off before I slit your throat."

A man's voice.

Coming right from beneath me.

I quickly rolled over, off of the man's body. In that moment, I realized I was alive, and insurmountable joy flooded me. When a man almost dies, and he comes to find he's still breathing, there is nothing more to be done but laugh. So I laughed. "You saved my life! Twice, now, I'd say!"

The man sat up. I couldn't see much in the dark, but I practically felt his anger wafting through the blackness that surrounded us. "I'm going to leave," he said, voice very low, "and you had best run very far away."

"Run away? Why?" I ran my hands lightly over my body, but a few more bumps and cuts from the fall hardly amounted to anything compared to my previous wounds.

The man stood without another word and began walking. He walked in the darkness, without a lantern or torch, as if he could see perfectly.

I stumbled after him, bare feet accustomed to the harsh terrain. "You won't answer me?" I asked.

The man, in response, said nothing. I followed him through complete darkness in silence.

He walked for hours — until the moon hung high above through the dense trees, and I only spotted glimpses of the beautiful ball of light every so often when we entered a meadow, and beyond the meadows, I saw very little. I couldn't see where I went, but I followed the man's light breathing and every so often, he stepped on something, and I followed the sound. I stepped on rocks, tripped on tree roots, ran into thorns, and tree branches slapped my face.

I felt like a forsaken lamb trying to chase a master that did not wish to be chased, but I had nothing more to lose.

After hours of walking, the man slowed and stopped in a small meadow beside a little creek. The sound of the creek made my heart soar, and I stumbled forward. "Water!" I grinned. "I haven't drank a drop all day—"

"Do not drink the water," the man said simply.

My shoulders fell and I stopped in the bushes beside him again. "Why?"

"You're foreign. It is unsafe for you." With that, the man began to set up camp. He had a pack on him, and he started a fire with a flintstone, feeding it some kindling before it took fully and lit up the little area. "Are you not a healer?"

I sighed. "I'm..." Desperate. And I could take medicine to cleanse myself later. But I was so thirsty *now*. "You're right." I turned back to him.

The man looked up, and his eyebrows furrowed slightly. "You're naked."

"Oh. Yes. I apologize..."

"I see. Your profession is not my concern." The man pulled a few woven baskets from his pack.

I winced, saying quickly, "It's nothing like that! I'm a priest."

The man eyed me again. "The northern priests are very strange, then."

I stepped closer, laughing at the absurdity of my situation. "No, no, er, I, well, I was robbed and stripped when I arrived here... That was last night, I suppose. Um, I'm Priest Bjorn, from the north, yes, but I usually wear clothes..."

The man shrugged slightly. "Put something on."

I laughed again. "It is a silly thing to me! Creator made us naked, and yet, we made it a great shameful thing."

"I do not particularly wish to see this." The man nodded once toward my groin, nonchalantly placing a small metal bowl over the fire, and opening the little baskets.

"I suppose I can find some leaves," a crooked grin escaped me, "as humanity did after the Split."

Once the food — was it rice? — simmered over the fire, the man pulled two pieces of clothing from his bag. "Here." He tossed them at me. "But do not bathe in the river. I'll boil water."

My joking manner ceased. "I can pay you back for the aid," I said firmly. "Whatever you need, say the word, please."

"I need nothing for clothes and boiling water." The man rolled his eyes and built the fire a bit up, then from the pack, he took a larger bowl, which, somehow, had been folded over, and filled it with water from the creek. He set the pot over the fire again.

I quickly pulled the tunic and pants on. Both items of clothing were too large for the man, but the shirt was baggy on me, and the pants fit, though were short around my ankles. I wondered where he had gotten clothes that did not fit him, and why he carried them around. But that didn't seem polite to ask, so instead, I said, "I didn't get your name."

"I didn't give it." The man stirred the rice on the fire and added some green-looking vegetables to it. It smelled heavenly already, but I hadn't eaten for two days.

"Ah," I said. "What is your name?"

The man's eyes cut at me again, as if I had asked some forbidden question. Perhaps the east was more hostile than I had even imagined. "Togo Furukawa," he said, tone ice cold. "But most call me Togo."

"Togo," I repeated. "It is an honor to meet you. Thank you for saving me before."

"*'A man must protect the innocent and the daft.'* I do not agree with the saying, but I had nothing to lose by saving the daft tonight." The man watched the food sizzle over the fire.

I laughed awkwardly. "I do appreciate it. Um, though, I must say, I am curious... of how things... turned out."

Togo gave no response, so I continued. "Why did the men flee when they heard you yell like that? You almost sounded like a berserker from my homeland."

Togo pulled a fold of bandages from his pack and shrugged. "I have never met a man that spoke so much."

I grimaced. "I mean... It is none of my business, I suppose." I dropped the topic.

The man let the water boil, and then said, "Sit and eat." He pulled the tin of heated food from the fire, using a wrapping of cloth, and used one spoon. We ate interchangeably, silent, and I savored every hot, blissful, spicy bite. Once we finished, the water in the pot boiled, and

Togo pulled it off. He let it cool slightly, then said, "I can patch the worst wounds."

"I appreciate it, but I can."

"You know how?" Togo frowned.

"I'm a priest, but I am also a man of medicine. And third, I am a firm believer that those two roles should always coincide." I reached for the small kit of medical supplies that Togo offered me.

"I forget how priests have so much to say," Togo said quietly.

I used the rags and clean water to cleanse the wounds, and then I stitched two of the gashes the thieves had given me. I didn't make a sound, and when I finished, I cleaned everything up again and offered to boil more water to clean the rags again.

Togo lit a pipe. He had watched me in silence, but I hadn't really noticed. I was, of course, too busy trying to stitch my arm and leg without needling any part that didn't need needling.

"All right," he said.

I got more water, and set it to boil over the fire, silent. I liked to talk. It helped me process things — and of course, it was a way to spread the love of Creator. But the blood loss, hunger, dehydration, and exhaustion settled in, and I didn't have much left in me.

I sat quietly, watching the orange and yellow flames lick at the pot.

Togo puffed smoke.

Cicadas sang in the night.

Every so often, something rustled or snapped in the trees.

I boiled the rags and hung them to dry on a bush. When the pots had been washed, too, and set aside, I turned to Togo. He said nothing, pulling a blanket from his pack. He threw it at me.

"I can't possibly take more—"

"I do not need it," he said, "but you are in a dangerous balance between illness and death."

Did he mean my wounds and exhaustion?

I straightened, indignant. "I am not so weak—"

Togo sat, laid down, and turned his back to me and the fire.

Biting my tongue, and trying to hold my temper, I laid down, too, and covered up with the blanket.

I strained to see the stars through the treetops above. The cool night hung heavy, and I pulled the blanket closer.

I had come here because Creator had told me to.

And I had not the slightest fledgling of an idea as to why, until I met Togo.

THREE

I woke early, and struggled to get the pot full of water at the creek.

Ashamedly, Togo's words were right: I was on the edge of being sick. The fact alone was humiliating — I was a big man, strong and tough, and my homeland wasn't exactly delicate. And yet, a beating and some cold was enough to make me want to curl up under a blanket for a while longer? That wouldn't do. The Letters told me to faint not: I couldn't be weak now.

I put more wood on the fire and placed the pot overtop so it would boil and we could have something to drink.

Togo sat up, studying me. "Fool."

"Good morning to you, as well," I said cheerfully. "Now, seeing I owe you for the help, supplies, and clothes, why don't we add food to that list again? I'm starving."

Togo frowned. "You cannot hunt?" "Well, with this limp, I think I would waste our time if I tried to," I admitted.

"Very well." He got up and stretched. "We'll use what rations I have left to save time."

"Save time?" I asked. "You're in a hurry to go somewhere?"

"Man is always in a hurry to go somewhere, even if they don't know where they're going," Togo mused.

I beamed. "You're wordy, for someone that isn't a priest."

Pulling the mini baskets woven of grass--no, it looked harder than grass--from his pack, Togo didn't acknowledge my jab. Was my sense of humor lost on a man of his culture? I didn't know what gaps lay between us, really.

"What is that?" I gestured to the baskets.

"Baskets. The north has them."

"The material looks different," I stressed. "It's very pretty."

Togo's expression hardened at my language. "It is bamboo."

I studied it, then exclaimed, "Is that what grows so much in the woods and at the port?"

Togo sighed heavily, as if I were a pettisome child. "You traveled to a foreign land with no previous knowledge of the land? Is that a wise thing for a priest to do?"

"No. Men of faith recommend against it," I said.

"I see."

I added, "I wish to learn. I do not wish to remain foolish and ignorant of this beautiful land."

Togo shrugged, stirring the rice and vegetables over the little pot. "You will not remain in this land long."

"Oh. Why not?"

"Do you remember what I told you?"

"Oh. What?"

Togo eyed me again. "Run away."

"Oh, that, yes, I remember. But I cannot run." I sat beside him, not too close, of course.

"You cannot run, but you do not have a purpose here, either." Togo tsked. "You are mad."

"I have a purpose. Why would you think I don't?" I demanded.

"I know a wandering soul when I see one," Togo said.

His words cut deep, far deeper than I wanted to admit, and I shoved them aside. "Creator led me here."

"You will die here."

"I have nothing to lose."

At that, Togo met my eyes again. He said nothing, but a mutual understanding was made between us: neither of us had anything to lose, and neither of us had anywhere drastic to go.

And when two souls of this nature meet, fate usually has them meet for a reason.

And they are usually scarcely removed from one another after they meet.

Togo pulled the bowl of food from the fire, and we shared another meal in silence, as the woods around us woke slowly.

WE TRAVELED ALL DAY through the woods, keeping far from the highway or paths. When I asked why we did this crude manner of travel, Togo replied, "It is safer."

I began to wonder if it was safer for us, or for others.

Togo had put our boiled water in a canteen, and we shared it throughout the day, but it wasn't enough, and I grew more sluggish as we continued on. I said nothing, but Togo must have known, because he said, "We'll come to a village soon."

When we came to the small, quiet village, Togo led me to a little mercantile. As we entered the wooden building, he said, "Do not speak or touch anything."

Feeling chastened, like a little child exploring the world for the first time, I replied, "Why not?" It was a sin, I knew, to argue, and I was supposed to agree quickly with my adversaries, as the Letters said, but I had trouble curbing my tongue around the man.

Togo didn't answer, and we went through the threshold — I had to lean down slightly to fit into the doorframe, and Togo barely walked beneath it. Tables and shelves lined the room, and I'd never seen some of the goods displayed before: spices, fabrics, and much more. I grew dizzy looking at everything and the smells of foreign foods and such hit me hard.

Togo approached the clerk at the counter. Togo's boots made no sound on the hardwood floors, but my bare feet slapped occasionally. I wondered how the man could walk so silently, and why he bothered to.

"We need rations," Togo said, pulling coins from his pocket and setting them on the table. The clerk eyed us both, but said nothing. He didn't even say, "Good morning!" or "What sort of rations?"

The clerk went into the back room. The mercantile was similar to the ones from my homeland. It just seemed smaller, and a lot smellier, but the smells were nice enough. They might have been better if I wasn't already on the verge of losing what little mind I had left.

I stared at a rack of horse tack. "Your people have very short horses."

Togo cut me a look.

I wasn't supposed to talk. I fell quiet again. Why was he so strict about that? Why couldn't I talk? Then again, the clerk had looked at me with, well, pure hatred. What had I done? Surely, word hadn't traveled that fast and far to inform the clerk I had been wandering naked on the highway? No, no, why would he hate me for a silly story like that?

I shook myself and Togo picked up one of the leather bridles. They were polished and smelled like the finest leather. He turned back to the counter as the clerk returned.

"Jun — does he still sell mounts?" Togo asked the clerk.

Frowning, the man nodded once. But he eyed me, and added promptly, "But he will not sell to a man like this." He handed over the sack of supplies without a word and took the coins from the countertop.

I bit my tongue. Of course, I was a different race — a complete foreigner here, but I hadn't quite expected this hostility, and I began to understand why Togo had told me to remain silent. I dropped my gaze for good measure.

Togo nodded and took the sack of supplies. He shouldered the bridle. The clerk gave me one last look of disgust before he hobbled into the back room again.

I followed Togo outside, breathing in the crisp air, mumbling, "Did I do something wrong?"

"You were born."

Grimacing, I asked, "Can I do anything to... help our current predicament?"

"Kill yourself."

Dare I say, the man had a sense of humor, even if it was not my own.

He walked down the street. I realized it was so quiet because people avoided us — I saw a rustle of fabric, a flash of movement, but every person that saw us coming down the dirt street quickly went inside or took another road around us. I sighed.

Togo stopped at a small smithy. A few men worked tirelessly in the little shop, the hammering and clanging of metal against metal making my feverish skull pound. The smells of smoke and dust clogged my nostrils.

Togo approached the smithy, saying under his breath, "Stay out of sight."

Confused, I obliged, and hid behind one of the little shops nearby the smithy. I tried to look around the corner beneath a few perfectly-placed barrels of... was that smell rum?

Togo entered the smithy. I didn't see much after that. I didn't hear much, either, though Togo's tongue changed to the local language. I had noticed many of the locals, like the trader on the highway, and Togo himself, knew my tongue, as well, but it definitely wasn't common. I didn't know much of the local language either — I had researched as much as I could before arriving here, but the eastern folks were private. Learning about their culture and language before arriving had been near impossible to do. They shared very little with the outside world.

Thus, probably why they despised me, too.

After about five minutes, Togo went to the back of the smithy. Sweat dripped down my forehead, but not because of the autumn sun — my fever was growing, and I couldn't combat it. After another five minutes, Togo returned to the street leading a mare by the new bridle he had purchased.

Now, the mare had no saddle, or any other tack, besides that beautiful bridle.

A lump swelled in my gut. I came out of hiding, hesitating. "What's her name?"

Togo's eyes narrowed. "You asked me for its name?"

"Well… Yes." I stroked the mare's neck. She was a larger horse than I had expected, with a sleek black coat. She was healthy, too, and her eyes were alert and wise.

Togo didn't answer again, and said, "Climb on."

I froze. "What?"

"You've ridden before?"

"Well, yes, but with a saddle…"

Togo huffed. "Climb on." He tied the pack around her neck so it hung loosely off her side, and then turned back to me. "Jump."

"Jump on." I repeated, insides squirming. "Right." I couldn't be a pissant now. Excuse me — it wasn't priestly-like to swear. I couldn't be a coward now. So I grabbed the mare's withers with shaky hands and swung upward. It was a ridiculous, clumsy motion, and I blamed it on my condition, but before I realized it, I was on the back of the horse.

However, my stomach twisted. A dreadful feeling came over me. I turned to the right and vomited what little breakfast I had all over the dirt.

Togo's face scrunched slightly, but then he pulled the mare forward. "If you fall, I will not go back for you," he said.

I believed him.

So I held on tightly with my hands and thighs. The mare's gait was smooth, but I could have ridden a cloud of silk and still jostled and lurched like a drunkard.

I was getting sicker, and I didn't understand it. Of course, exhaustion, dehydration, and a beating could do such to a man. But this sickness felt worse than what I had faced before. My head grew fuzzy, my vision blurred, and I couldn't stop sweating.

I struggled to stay on the mare. I struggled to breathe. I struggled to keep my stomach contained. And I struggled to understand why Creator had allowed me in such a position. How badly had I failed Him? He must be ashamed at how far off His mission I had fallen.

Then again, I didn't even know what the mission was.

After about a mile, Togo stopped the mare in a small meadow. He said, very matter-of-factly, "You were poisoned."

"What?" I slurred.

"The arrow wound." Togo reached up and dragged me off the mare. He didn't cushion my fall, and allowed me to fall into the dusty grass. "The tip of the arrow was poisoned. It was not a hostile village, and you are lucky they do not have very trained warriors."

I sat up weakly, groaning. "That wasn't hostile? They fired at me. And hit me."

"You are still alive." Togo shrugged. He left me in the clearing, and led the mare to the little stream nearby. He continued, "The medicine I purchased will help."

"You let us walk a mile before you told me this?" I rubbed my face.

"You rode. I walked."

"Am I going to die?" I didn't fear death, but I wasn't particularly fond of the idea of dying this way, either.

Togo spat. "You are a little schoolgirl."

"I think my question is justified!"

He brought the mare over and tied her to a tree. He rummaged through the pack and retrieved a small vial. He opened it, and shoved the mixture toward me. "Drink."

I took the vial with shaking hands. The poultice was black and tasted foul, but I downed all of it. I tossed the vial back at Togo. "There."

He caught it with surprisingly ease and placed it in the pack again. "Now, sleep."

"For how long? Are you going to leave me here?" I asked. "I can sleep on the horse. You can tie me to her and we can go."

Togo grunted. "I'm in no hurry."

Not exactly comforting, or answering my questions, but I succumbed.

My boiling blood pounded in my ears. I rubbed my aching eyes, and then passed out in the dirt without another word.

A SCREAM WOKE ME.

It pierced the woods like a hawk's screech across a valley.

"Let me go, bastard!"

There it was again. I blinked a few times, then lifted my head. It felt like a log, but my vision was clearer. From the fire's light, I saw a bit in the night around me.

A short woman, in a torn, bloody white dress, hit Togo with a club-like stick. Togo deflected the blow, and just stood still, his face unreadable in the firelight.

It looked like a ghost fighting a ghoul.

"Let go!" the woman cried again.

Togo wasn't even holding her. In that moment, I recognized the tone of her voice. It was rage, and a berserk-like rage at that, but something more.

Fear.

And pain.

Togo perhaps heard the same, because he didn't touch the woman.

I sat up weakly, coughing. "H-hello!" I intervened. "Please desist from hitting my partner!"

The woman whirled. She had long brown hair, and her complexion and face were similar to my own — she wasn't a local. That was clear.

She swung her club at me, instead, her bare, bloody feet stepping over the campground in a blur. The stick almost bashed me, but like a cougar, Togo leapt forward. He grabbed the weapon and threw it into the woods as quick as a blink. I gaped. How had he done that so fast? The woman hadn't even had time to fight him over it.

Screaming, the woman whirled at Togo again. "Give me the money and I'll go!"

Money? So she was a thief? No, that didn't seem quite right — why was she still fighting for money if she were a normal thief? Thieves came in the night and took without a battle, and if caught, they fled.

I stood on wobbly legs — the antidote to the poison had taken effect, and I could see better, and think a bit clearer, although this situation was enough to baffle me on a good day. "Stop!" I cried. "Please! We want to help!" I held up my hands so the woman could see I had no ill will. I mean, I didn't even have a weapon.

"We?" Togo glared at me across the woman's small frame.

The woman stepped back, stumbling a little on some rocks. She clenched her fists, as if preparing to fight us both single-handedly. "I need the money!" she repeated.

Blood poured down a gash from her round face. Her lip was busted. She walked with a slight limp, and the blood staining most of her white dress looked to be her own, but I couldn't see any huge, bleeding wound elsewhere on her body. What had the woman faced? What was going on?

"Why do you need the money?" I asked. "Perhaps we can help—"

"She is fleeing," Togo said, "and in vain."

The woman snarled. "I killed the bastard that took me. Don't make me kill you, too!"

Kill? The bastard that took her? I tensed, stepping forward. "There's no need for that," I said firmly. "You're hurt. We can help."

"We cannot." Togo shook his head. "Her master will come for her."

"He's dead!" The woman glanced at our packs. Her eyes darted to the horse, too.

Creator, I had never seen such desperation before.

Togo scoffed, but I cut in. "We'll give you money, but if Togo is correct, then men will hunt you, yes? You won't get very far alone when you're injured. Please, let us help."

I ignored Togo's expression.

The woman hesitated again. Then her shoulders slumped. "I—"

Before she could speak, Togo hissed, "Silence." In a flash, Togo had killed the fire with dust, and pushed the woman and I behind the bushes beside the mare. Togo grabbed the mare's bridle.

In the darkness, I saw nothing, but after a long moment, I heard voices from afar.

How had Togo heard those voices long before I had?

I held my breath. The woman crouched to my left, and Togo remained to my right with the mare, and we kept silent, even our breathing strained.

If the men looking for the woman were hostile, I wasn't sure if we could make it very far. But I would fight, if I must. I couldn't let a woman be harmed.

Footsteps followed, and the slap and crunch of branches and twigs came like a choir. The group of men came close

— they were just beyond the meadow. We were hidden in the shadows, but if they swerved their lanterns too far, they would see the mare, and we would be displayed.

But the voices, spoken in a language I couldn't understand, eventually dulled. The lantern lights vanished.

The men had continued on.

I reached over once it had been silent for a while. "See, Miss?" I asked. "We'll help you —"

But when I looked down, the woman had slumped forward into the dirt and leaves, unconscious. I quickly lifted her upright, panic rising. She had lost much blood. And what if she had been poisoned or something? What could I do?

Togo swore beside me. "Fool."

FOUR

I MANAGED TO GET the woman onto the mare after tending her wounds, and Togo and I walked in silent through the night. My bare feet grew sore, and my body, still recovering from the poison, ached, but I didn't slow down.

By morning, we had covered a good amount of ground. Togo entered a small village alone and purchased a pair of men's clothes for the woman. He didn't say a word, and we continued onward.

But we were headed south: toward the port, where I had come from. As Togo cooked us breakfast over a small fire, and I tended the woman's wounds again, I asked, "Where are we going?"

"*We?*" Togo said.

"Well, yes."

"I was not aware there was a *we*."

"Are we going to the ports?" I finished wrapping the woman's head. Her face and arms were all freckled, but I didn't look at much beyond that as I changed her out of the gown and into the tunic and trousers. Togo didn't look up from his cooking.

"You are."

"Oh. And you?"

Togo shrugged. "A wise man never tells where he is headed."

"Why am I going to the port, then?" I frowned in dismay.

"You'll be killed here."

"I cannot leave," I said firmly. "Creator led me here. I must find why, and fulfill my purpose."

Togo tsked and said nothing more.

"You cannot force me to take a ship." I gently covered the woman—now cleaned and fully clothed—with our one and only blanket.

"I can force you to leave me alone," Togo threatened.

"I've yet to repay you for your aid," I argued.

Togo eyed the woman. "For a man trying to repay his debts, you continue to collect them."

"What were we supposed to do!" I scowled. "Leave her there? She would have been captured." I changed course. "Who was after her, anyway? You know, don't you? What was going on?"

Togo sat beside me then, and we ate from our bowl, but we left an equal portion for the woman when she would wake. "She was purchased as a slave. Are you so dense you did not see that?"

"I... I figured as much," I said, "but the gown... I mean... was she... purchased as a concubine? Does this culture allow that? I read it was a very honorable culture..." Disgust welled in my throat, and I forced some rice down, looking at my feet.

"There are no honorable cultures. There are only men, and men are good and bad." Togo finished his portion like a ravenous dog. "If the woman killed her master, she would have been stoned. It is a miracle she escaped."

Dare I say, the man sounded impressed by the woman's slaughter.

I was, too.

"She's not very big," I mumbled. "It must have been terrifying for her to do such a thing."

"She is a fighter." Togo shook his head, as if that explained everything. "She is from your land, yes?"

"I... think so, yes, though her accent is heavier than my own, so perhaps she was further south than Norkid." I sighed. "Anyway, if she was enslaved, I am sure she'll want to return home."

Togo grunted without responding. It would have been better conversation to discuss the mortality of man with a blade of grass.

"So we should take her home," I prompted.

Togo eyed me then, setting the empty bowl aside. He licked his fingers. I waited for some sort of reply, but he gave none, so I continued, "Well?"

"I am sure you can handle the expedition when you return to Norkid."

I rubbed the bridge of my nose. "I'm not returning to Norkid to stay. I'll take this girl home and then return here, as Creator told me to."

"You are a stubborn fool."

I was supposed to be slow to anger, so I said, "Where are you going, anyway? I'm beginning to think you're some sort of mercenary, yes? Then, perhaps, could I pay you to accompany us to Norkid?"

Togo's expression darkened and he eyed me as if I had asked him to skin himself alive. "What?"

"Could I pay you —"

"You could not afford me," Togo cut me off.

"Well, not currently. But I have savings in my home village — I could pay you when we arrived." I still tried to keep my frustration hidden. I needed to be patient. Show a good testimony. All of that.

"You could not afford me."

"Well, name the price."

Togo scoffed.

"Well, you're already escorting me to the port," I said. "Why? You aren't worried for my safety. So I assume you're already going to the port, and I'm merely following. Where will you go beyond the shore?"

"It is never a wise thing to ask a man where he is roaming."

"I'm a fool," I said, "and my God led me here, so I've nothing to lose by continuing to forsake man's concepts and pursue Creator's path, no matter how ludicrous it may make me appear."

"You follow your own whims in naivety."

"Why don't you just tell me where you're going?" I insisted. "Perhaps I could even help? I still owe you for saving my life twice."

"If you want to repay me for saving your life, leave me alone." Togo pulled his pipe and filled it. His fingers were deft, nimble.

It made my insides twist when I realized that Togo had not denied my claims of him being a mercenary.

Was he?

Or was he only ignoring me, as usual?

No. Something told me that my assumption was genuine. Discernment was not necessarily a blessing from Creator I bore, but I sought after it, and if I had finally discerned something correctly, well... Damn. It wasn't what I had wanted to discern correctly.

"I can't do that," I said. "I need to repay the debts. And, well, I think we need to help this woman, too."

"I have no master," he said pointedly.

"Partners, then? I can pay," I persisted.

Togo puffed smoke from his pipe. "You do not know who I am. So I shall allow this insult to pass by."

The way the man said it made my skin crawl. He was doubtlessly a mercenary, but he must have been more, too. It made sense: the clerk at the shop had been so sober. The smithy men had been so willing to sell him a steed. The warriors in the village had fled at the sound of the beast.

Was he some sort of legendary killer?

I gulped. Well, Creator could change any sort of man. I wouldn't fear this one just because of what he was. I still owed him debts.

We said nothing, and in that moment, the woman woke.

FIVE

I TURNED TO THE woman and said, "Hello!" But got nothing more out of my mouth before the woman sat up, swinging. Her fist collided with my nose, and I jerked back.

Before she could throw her other fist into my face, I exclaimed, "I'm sorry! You're safe! Wait!"

The woman froze, both fists clenched still, with wide, piercing eyes staring through me like shards of glass. I added, "You're safe. We helped, remember?"

She probably didn't recall much — she had passed out during the heat of the hunt, after all. She glanced between me and Togo, then took a shaky breath. "It's..."

"I'm Priest Bjorn," I said, flashing a smile. "And this is my partner, Togo. You found us in the woods last night, and we got you away from the men that were after you. Here, now, are you hungry? We saved you breakfast."

The woman glanced down at herself, but Togo spoke before she could make a move. "We have not touched you. The priest changed your clothes so you wouldn't catch your death in the cold."

Heat flooded my face, and I added hastily, "I didn't see anything! I apologize for being so, uh, improper, but you were bloody and cold, and I only wished to ensure you were unharmed. I'm a healer — as well as a priest."

The woman slowly glanced down again, jaw tight. She mumbled, "Right."

"What's your name?" I asked. I got her bowl of food ready and handed it over.

"Maude," the woman murmured. She met my gaze with weary eyes. "You... both have no idea what you've done... the men will continue to hunt me —"

"They might, but they won't succeed." Togo stood.

Maude eyed him with a frown. "How so?"

Togo didn't answer and bridled the horses. I offered a weak smile. "Togo is a very skilled warrior. Anyone that tries to harm you will quickly realize their error. Now, you escaped slavery, yes? I apologize — I do not mean to be forward, but we've no time to waste, yes?"

The woman gulped down food, eyes downcast. "Aye."

"I don't want to press. I understand you're in a very difficult situation. But you can join us, yes? We're going to the port. We can return you home, if you wish."

The woman stiffened. "What?" she asked, looking up. She couldn't have been any older than I was. She seemed much older, though. Well, maybe it was because she had tried to kill us when we first met. "Who are you both to offer that? Mercenaries? Traders? Listen, *Priest*, I won't be sold again —"

"We're not traders!" I said in dismay. "Truly!"

"If we were, we would have tied you up and wouldn't feed you." Togo eyed the woman.

The woman's eyes flashed. "You little —"

"Please, let's not argue," I intervened. "We're as we say we are. We're going to the port already. We wouldn't mind if you joined us. It would be safer for you, too."

I noticed Togo's left eye twitching. I ignored it.

The woman forced the rest of her food down, dropping her head. "I cannot pay." She shoved the bowl at me. "I can't even pay for the food. Or the clothes. Or —"

"Neither can I," I said quickly. "I am repaying my debts to Togo as we speak. Well, at least, I'm going to. Why don't you join us? We can work our debts off together, yes?"

Togo's eye twitched again. Perhaps, as a healer, I should check that tic out.

"How much would it cost?" Maude jutted her chin at us. "Perhaps I would be better off dying than indebting my life forever."

I laughed. "Life is always worth living, even in the harshest of conditions!" I put out the fire carefully. "A debt of the flesh is nothing to ruin your soul over. Believe me, I ought to understand —" I caught myself, and flashing a smile, added, "Besides, Togo wouldn't charge a lady for his aid. It wouldn't be right." I gave Togo a look. "Isn't that correct, Togo?"

Eyes narrowing, Togo said, "I am allowed to speak now?" The sarcasm in his tone bit.

Maude sat up a bit straighter. Her pale face flickered. "Well, the port is where I need to go to escape this godforsaken land. I'll try to pay for my fare, at least, does that sound fair?" She looked toward Togo, and not me, but I glanced at him, too.

After all, if the man wanted to, he could have killed us in our sleep by now, or run during the night, but he hadn't. I was curious as to why — but didn't dare ask, after the record I was already setting for myself.

Togo didn't answer for a moment. When he did, all he said was, "I suppose."

"It's settled then," I said firmly. We're going to the port."

SIX

Maude talked more openly than I had expected. I talked with her, but during the days of travel, Togo said very little, almost nothing. I tried to invite him into some of the conversations but he never bit.

Maude told me that she came from a good, prosperous village outside of the Bour Mountains, and her people had traded with Norkid often. Maude was a poet, though she hardly spoke like one.

I had expected a poet to be eloquently spoken, and wise and solemn. Mauda was solemn at times, but stumbled over her words sometimes, and often chased multiple trails of thoughts in one conversation. Of course, this did not bother me, and I found her company and discussion quite enjoyable, especially after being with Togo for days of very little genuine conversation.

As we drew closer to the port, Maude grew more trusting. She even began cooking the evening meals, and told us stories. It was admirable — I could not quite imagine being in her shoes and still putting on a brave face and telling stories of courageous heroes and heroines she had met, or even retelling stories from the Letters with such gumption and heart that I felt, as a priest, I was being transferred to times of old like never before.

Even still, Maude always finished her tales with a humble, "I could write it more beautifully," she would say, and add, "And I'm sorry for stumbling over parts of it." As if we would beat her for the mismatched words or occasional bouts of discussion mid-story.

I found her ways amusing, but mostly, almost heartbreaking. What stories did she contain that she hid? Why did she apologize for such trifling things? Why was she so happy — even so far from home, after being enslaved and killing a man for her freedom? I think most women, even men, would have been broken souls.

But she did not seem broken.

Though I think she still was, in a sense. I think some of us are just better at hiding it than others. And we're usually the ones that keep hiding it, because no one sees, or cares, until we break so much that there's nothing left, and then we keep going anyway because we must.

I knew this, and accepted this fate, but as I watched Maude finish her tale that night, under the vast sky of stars, I decided I didn't want the fate for Maude.

Of course, I barely knew the woman, and had no place to direct her life or fate.

I said a brief prayer over our meal. Togo, as usual, waited till we finished, but wasn't listening to the prayer. We ate in silence, and when we finished, Maude gathered our plates. Togo went off to the creek to gather us water. Maude put the pot on the fire to boil, watching Togo return to the creek. He sat against a tree and watched the waters, smoking his pipe in the darkness.

I helped Maude wash the dishes in the hot water when it finished boiling.

"Maude?" I asked. "May I ask something?"

"Of course." She scrubbed the last bowl without looking up. Her long hair hung around her face, and she hunched over her bowl like it might flee from her.

"You've mentioned Creator, and you tell the stories from the Letters more passionately than many priests," I began. Glancing down at my own bowl as I wiped it dry, I asked, "But... it is almost as if you hide behind the stories."

Maude jerked her head up. "What do you mean?"

"Well..." I didn't look up. "It's as if you speak the stories of the Letters as if you believe them, but as if they're still only stories..." But who was I to assume sadness, or brokenness, or pain, behind the poet's beautiful stories? Only, I knew better. Stories were told the strongest from the most broken of voices.

Maude finished washing the bowl and handed it to me. I dried it carefully, remaining silent as I waited for her response. Would she be angered? I shouldn't pry. Only, I didn't mean to pry. I wanted to help. To understand.

I did not want to lose another soul — of course, I understood it was not my doing, or deeds, that saved souls, but I wanted to look back upon my life, when I died, which was inevitably soon at the rate I was going, and know I had loved greatly, and had never let a soul pass me by without *seeing* it.

Maude finally spoke. She looked into the woods, as if seeing through the pitch black trees and shrubs, her expression soft. "Aye, I suppose there's truth to that," she said.

I tensed. "Oh..."

"It is easier to tell a story and believe the truth in a story, than to tell the truth and to believe the truth alone." Maude's piercing blue eyes met mine, and she gave a weary smile, the weight of a thousand lives behind those eyes. "So I tell stories, and I tell them to encourage others, but mostly, I think, I tell them to give myself a reason to be, too. I tell them to remind myself of the truth, and I tell them to help others. I have, then, only two reasons to be here, yes? Is that not sad? Terribly pathetic. But it is true. I'm sorry to be so forward — but you are a priest, and I hope you can handle my rudeness." And just like that, Maude's mask returned, and her heaviness left, and her smile brightened like plaster. "I—"

I stopped her then. "Why do you apologize so much?" I asked. Then, catching my bluntness, I added, "Of course, I can handle your honesty. I welcome it, truly." I dried the last spoon and shoved the dishes back into our pack, continuing, "But you do not have to apologize to me, and you do not have to lie... about anything."

Maude's expression tightened and she looked down at her hands. "I suppose it would be a sin to lie to a priest," she mused.

"Truly," I said firmly, "if I can help in any way—"

Maude shook her head quickly, but just as she opened her mouth, a sharp sound pierced the air, and a flash of black filled my eyes.

I PUSHED MAUDE TO the ground, shielding her with my body as the ambush broke out.

Togo had rushed between us and the forest like a cougar, and one arrow — intended for me — had stuck in Togo's shoulder, but he rushed into the thicket. Yells and cries followed.

I pinned Maude on the dirt as more arrows fell around us. I didn't have a weapon, but I reached across Maude and grabbed a large stick from the burning fire.

When the arrows faltered, I jumped up, running toward the woods. "Hide, Maude!" I yelled — of course, where she would hide, or could hide, I didn't know — and plunged into the bushes with the burning stick.

A small group of men, clad in all black, fought Togo. It was like a group of rats pissing off a wolf — their bows were all snapped on the forest floor, and their blades struck against Togo's katanas, but they never hit his body.

Togo wielded his katanas like they were an extension of his own arms. In seconds, he sliced through two men, and their screams echoed in the dark night.

I hit one of the men with the burning stick. To my chagrin, his black coat set fire. I immediately pushed him down, hoping that would stop the fire.

Togo cut down another man. I realized, again, that he killed ruthlessly, as if the bloodshed of man mattered as much as the bloodshed of a rodent or pest. My stomach twisting, I lunged again and struck one of the men that swung at Togo with his blade.

The man stumbled, and Togo whirled, cutting the man down dead. I winced. "Togo! We don't have to kill them —"

Two men remained, and one jumped me. His knife flashed in the light of my makeshift torch weapon.

I froze up. Every fiber of my being seized.

The forest, the darkness, the yells, the smell of blood, everything around me disappeared, replaced by a memory I had tried to forget.

A broken window. A small, cold room. A giant arm, coming down, down, down. Hot skin against mine. Sobs echoing in the room — my own, and hers, too.

Pain. Pain. Hot, fiery pain. Then everything was cold.

And —

"Bjorn!" a woman's voice screamed through the forest.

I jerked forward.

The bandit's knife nicked my neck, just as Togo tumbled into the man, sending him flying. Togo slit the man's throat before I could sit up. I yelled anyway: "Togo, stop!" even though it was too late.

The body fell back, blood spurting. Togo stood swiftly and turned to me. He held his katanas. Silent.

"You didn't have to kill them all," I choked.

"They purchase women like cattle," Togo said simply. "This is the injustice your God kills nations over, is it not?"

I stumbled to my feet. "You're not Creator. We cannot just slaughter them —"

"You wanted to save the woman." Togo cut me off, voice cold as ice. "If you are not prepared to defend her life, you should kill her now and be finished."

My blood boiled. My vision blurred. How could he say such things? But then again, he was partially correct. I had promised Maude that we would protect her. How could I do that while struggling to fight when I needed to?

How could Creator be pleased with my cowardly heart?

"Togo!" Maude hissed. "That's not true!" She hushed the mercenary as a child might hush a play rag doll.

I half-expected Togo to turn and strike her, but he merely eyed her without argument.

Maude stormed over, glancing at the corpses at our feet. "I don't want more bloodshed because of me!" Her voice rose, panic in her pale face. "I don't want anyone else to die, Togo!"

"If you wish to live, it must be so." Togo turned away. He sat at the campfire and began cleaning his wound and katanas, as if nothing had happened.

How could he carry the weight of those he killed like flies? Or did he feel any burden at all?

I couldn't outrun the blood on my hands. And Togo acted as if killing were as necessary as breathing.

"I'm sorry..." I dropped my head as Maude stepped over to me. "Are you hurt?" I asked.

Maude took one of my hands and squeezed it tightly. "Thank you for protecting me. I'm sorry it's endangered you both. I didn't think they would continue the hunt..."

"You do not need to apologize," I said, giving her hand a squeeze in return. "We're partners now. It's to be expected." I glanced at the corpses briefly before mumbling, "I should... bury them..."

"We're moving out tonight," Togo spoke up from the fireside, "it isn't safe if there are more men coming. We'll go to the port tonight and buy a room at the inn."

I cringed and Maude didn't release my hand. "But —"

"It will be a long night of travel, but we can make it. It's safest." Togo didn't look over.

I led Maude to the fire. She sat stiffly, as if in a sudden trance, and stared into the flames. I said, standing nearby, "Why would they still be after her, even now?"

"They must have paid a good penny." Togo shrugged. He finished patching the arrow wound on his shoulder, and sheathed his cleaned katanas. "If that is so, we shouldn't waste more time fighting whatever troops they send."

"Troops?" I hesitated. "You mean they.. the ones that have fought us... aren't just villagers?"

Maude's head ducked. Her hands shook and rubbed against her knees — a visible sign of a soul under distress.

"Tell him, Maude." Togo stood and began packing the camp.

I glanced at Maude, confusion growing. "What's wrong?"

"T-the village leader purchased me," she said weakly. "I... I-I killed the clan's chief..."

A heavy exhale escaped me. "Oh. That does... make sense. Well, we'd best be off then." I offered her a hand to help her stand.

Maude gaped at my hand, her eyes filling with tears. "A-aren't you angry? Won't you make me leave now? You could both go and let them find me —"

"Don't be a fool," I said. I flashed a smile. "We're partners now! We've got a journey ahead of us, don't we? Now, you did the just thing, and Creator sees that, so I think He'll bless our endeavors. Let's go along, then."

Maude grabbed my hand, her small hand shaking in my own. "I didn't want to say the truth in case you changed your mind... I-I am sorry..."

"What have you to be sorry for? As I said, you committed a great act of justice. It is to be applauded." I guided her to the mare. I bridled Bear, the mount, quickly. "Now, mount, yes?" I finished helping Togo pack in a frenzy. In moments, we had packed, killed the fire, and Togo had stripped the corpses of a few coins. I didn't stop him from stealing, though it made my stomach stir.

And then we were off. Maude rode Bear, and Togo and I trodded alongside the mare on either side, heading into the thick, cool night as owls hooted and bugs chirped.

SEVEN

By dawn, we arrived at the small, bustling port at the sea's edge. Maude sat on Bear, practically hunched over the horse's neck now. It was at that moment, when I looked up and peered into her face, that I saw pain in her eyes — not mental pain, though I am sure she still mourned the deaths she thought she had caused. But the pain in her eyes was physical.

Had she been harmed during the fight last night? No, no, she hadn't, I had checked, and even if she had been hurt without me seeing it, she would have mentioned it, and we would have had to patch her.

So why did Maude look to be in pain?

"Is everything all right?" I whispered to her. Maude glanced down at me, a weak smile coming to her chapped lips.

"Aye. Of course."

I knew a lie when I heard one. Well, usually I did, anyway. I did for certain this time.

Togo didn't let me push further, and he said, "We're not too late to board a ship. Hurry."

We walked along at the mare's sides, and I wiped sweat that dripped at my temples, despite the cool morning air. The sun was rising higher, but a cool fog still sat over the port. It made my heart soar to see the ocean again — the vast, blue waters that beckoned me closer. Of course, I must follow wherever Creator led, and I didn't know if my journey here was over, but a detour was surely from Creator, since He had put Maude in our path. Either way, no matter where I went, traveling the seas in the interim made it all worth it.

The crisp smell of the ocean hit me as we neared the docks. I fought a grin. Now was not the time to let my excitement control me. The situation at hand was, after all, quite serious. Maude was in danger, and the men hunting us could appear again at any time — well, their backup, that was — and Togo could possibly leave us at any point. I couldn't tell if he was going to vanish on us or not. I hoped not.

"It's a lovely port." Maude's voice barely slipped over the breeze. "How strange to think so many terrible things have happened here."

Her words struck my chest, and I cast a wary glance at Togo. Of course, I had faced troubles in this land, but it was absolutely nothing compared to what Maude had faced.

Yet, the pain in her eyes was more than fear of what might happen to her. Still, I could not pinpoint exactly what the pain was.

Togo led us to the docks. He promptly told Maude to dismount as a few sailors eyed us from the long, wooden dock. Ships, small and big ones, foreigners' and local fishermen's, lined the docks. One of the locals approached Togo and spoke in his tongue.

Togo responded. I kept Maude close, and she stood stiffly. I worried if her injuries were internal, and perhaps she was still suffering from the predicament with her previous master — but surely, if that were the case, she would be exhibiting more signs by now.

The local man frowned at me and Maude, then eyed Togo. He nodded and took the mare, shoving coins into Togo's hands. The merchant gave a bow — what a strange thing to do, but then again, perhaps Togo really was a legendary mercenary, and if so, respect was surely owed — and hurried off with our horse.

My chest fell. "I didn't get to say goodbye to —"

"This is enough for a fare." Togo turned toward the ships.

Maude hurried after me. "I'll pay it back," she said weakly, "all of it."

"Aye, we shall," I agreed. I offered a reassuring smile, the salty breeze ruffling my shaggy hair. "In no time at all!"

Maude's expression softened slightly, and she kept her head down, focusing on her steps so she didn't run into me or teeter too close to the edge of the dock. Togo finally slowed at a large foreign ship. It wasn't one from my homeland, but it was still larger than the eastern ships surrounding it. The name on the bow of the ship read *Sinner*.

I gulped. "Do we know who this belongs to?"

"Captain Skebok." Togo approached the gangplank. He seemed just at home among the ships as he did in the woods, too.

"Uh, where is he from?" I asked.

"Does it matter?" Togo stepped onto the gangplank.

I swallowed my other questions and waited on the dock with Maude.

A short man with short black hair and sideburns approached Togo. He rubbed his mustache as he nodded at him. "The legend himself, aye? What can I help you with?" How could a greeting sound so threatening at the same time? Did the captain think that Togo was there to cause trouble? I cringed.

Maybe I should have tried talking to the captain. Then again, I didn't have the money for the fare.

"We have money for three fares," Togo said. "We can go as far as you can take us." While he was civil, he certainly wasn't begging, either. I couldn't expect too much gratitude from Togo, that was certain.

The captain cast a glance toward Maude and I. "Slaves?" he asked Togo. "I didn't think you were one for sexual pleasures, Black Angel."

"Clients," Togo said.

The captain's bushy eyebrows shot up. "Clients?" He laughed. "These two? They do not look like they can afford you."

"Do you have room for three on *Sinner*?" Togo asked. Nothing ever fazed him. He continued right along.

"Aye, aye. Anything for you." Captain Skebok waved a hand. "Come aboard."

I followed Togo onto *Sinner* with Maude holding onto my arm, and thus, we began the next part of our journey, a step into the unknown that inevitably, only God could understand or foresee. But such was life.

PART II

ONE

The ship was a trader's ship, but the crew was unlike any lot I had ever met.

Captain Skebok was from Farsik, a well-educated man that spoke like a ghetto rat, and he spoke very little of his past, but I gleaned enough from his crew's gossip that he had raised himself in the Farsik gallows, and eventually found himself taken in by a wealthy family, who trained him up in differing trades until the man eventually went to the sea. He had started his own trading business off of basic goods, and had grown into one of the most luxurious tradesmen at sea. He traded fabrics, foods, and other things, but we weren't, of course, able to see much of the goods, since they had been traded at the eastern port.

The first mate was a thin man, a bit taller than Skebok, with long blond hair in thick locks, with freckles covering every inch of his skin. Berkeley's eyes were green, greener than the grasses in Norkid during the summertime, and saw every little thing that occurred on the ship.

Captain Skebok was a loose-leader. He laughed, chatted, and led the crew with high spirits. He still reminded me of a child playing in the streets as if nothing in the world truly mattered. Of course, he had to have some sort of responsibility in him, since his business was so prolific, but it did not show.

However, perhaps that was why he had Berk at his side. Berk kept the men in line when they drank too much or didn't apply themselves enough in their daily work.

Berk did not seem so frivolous in spirit, and so he quickly took to speaking with Maude and I every night, after the long days of sailing. I worked alongside Togo with the crew. Maude worked in the kitchen, but she sat on the deck most of the time, and watched us — there was little to be done in the kitchen, as they already had a chef handling the grunt work — and told us stories.

I asked for the first story. I asked her to remind me of the parable in the Letters about the shepherd's rod. Maude obliged, but she wove a tale possibly more emotional than the Letters themselves.

We worked, but as the cool winds chapped our lips, and our bones ached from the rough sailing, Maude's stories gave us morale.

And by the end of the week, the crew would ask Maude for another tale, even if I was not around.

I knew this, because Maude told me.

She stopped in the hall below the ship's deck. I was going to the crew's bunkroom, where I slept with Togo and the others. Maude had a small cot in a storage room, but she didn't complain. It scared me to think of sleeping in some cramped, musty room all alone, but she preferred the privacy, and I didn't blame her for that.

"They're asking for more stories." Maude beamed. "I'm so glad I know many of them by heart."

"Perhaps you could tell them one of your own tales, too?" I suggested. Her eyes glinted in the light of the lantern hanging on the wall nearby. "I've enjoyed the stories you've told me so far."

"I speak my own stories better through a pen," Maude said hastily.

"You're aboard a ship of men that have received little to no education, and have nothing to do all day but sweat under the cruel elements, drink, and sleep," I said dryly. "I think a story, in any form or display, would be greatly welcomed."

Maude glanced down at the floor, shrugging slightly. "Perhaps. Um, have you spoken much to Togo since we boarded the ship? It's been a week, and he's hardly spoken to me. I am... just worried..."

"He is a man of very few words." I tilted my head. "Is something wrong?"

"I want to repay my debt," Maude said firmly. She glanced up at me then. "I do not want to live in debt. To either of you."

"You owe me nothing," I blurted. "Nothing at all. Please, we're friends, yes? That's all I ask of you."

Maude's lips scrunched together. She did that when she was uncertain, I had noticed. "No one means that."

"How can I prove myself, then?" I furrowed my eyebrows. "I do mean it. I want nothing. But friendship, that is, and if you choose not to be my friend, well, I'll respect that too, and return you safely home regardless."

"You're a strange man," Maude mused, huffing slightly. "But I suppose I must take your word."

"As for Togo, don't worry about him," I added. "I'll handle it."

"He doesn't want us to repay him," Maude mumbled, "but I can't live in debt..."

"I'll handle it." I nodded. "Now, Miss Maude, please sleep well, and may Creator bless you with pleasant dreams."

Maude smiled, told me goodnight, and slipped into the storage room. I hurried into the bunk room, which was already piled up with men sleeping in hammocks like a flock of birds perched for the night. I changed from my dirty, sweaty clothes, and said my prayers on the floor. The crewmates gave me a respectful distance. I didn't think any were really Believers in Creator, but I talked openly about my faith, and prayed quietly so as not to disturb their peace, either.

Then I hopped into my hammock. I nearly fell out of it, but I was getting the hang of it. Finally.

Minutes later, as snores surrounded me from the crew, the door opened and Togo slid inside. I glanced over. "Togo?" I whispered.

Togo went to his hammock. It was right above me.

"Togo?" I whispered again.

He glanced down but said nothing.

"What were you doing?" I sat up a little, grunting. "Is everything all right?"

"Yes." He removed his tunic.

"Could we discuss our plan?" I asked, rubbing my head tiredly. "Maude is worried —"

"She should be."

"What? Why?"

"You're both very stupid. Idiocy is a worrisome thing."

I scowled up at Togo. But I was supposed to be slow to wrath. "We only want to pay the debt we owe you. You saved our lives. Is it so stupid of us to want to aid you in return?"

Togo dropped down slightly, till his head wasn't far from mine, and his dark eyes flashed. He said, very quietly, so only I could hear, "Do you still not understand who I am?"

The men in the hammocks around us slept and snored. My heart rang in my ears.

"I know you're a mercenary. A good one," I said slowly.

"I do not need the aid of a priest or a peasant," Togo whispered coldly.

"Then what about the help from two friends?" I insisted.

"You are the most stubborn man I've ever had the misfortune of meeting," Togo hissed and straightened slightly.

"It's the good Creator in me," I said, "now, how about it? Like it or not, we have debts to you, and we can't allow it to go unfulfilled. It's not right of us."

But more than that — Togo was why I had come east. And Maude.

These two souls, one saved, and one seemingly forsaken, were my only real excuse to live on — and I could not let either escape me.

Of course, I couldn't say this to anyone, but it was what tossed and turned in my gut.

I needed them, yes. I needed to fulfill Creator's will, and I believed this was it. These two people needed Creator's compassion.

Perhaps, as selfish as it was to think even for a moment, but just perhaps they needed me, too.

"Hm." Togo changed his clothes, piling his dirty clothes into his pack like usual. We were on a ship in the middle of the ocean, and he still kept his possessions in the pack, as if he might vanish someplace.

I waited a moment longer for his response. Togo looked down at me again, expression difficult to read, and he said quietly, "Fine. We'll take the woman to her homeland, and then the debt is paid."

I hesitated. "But that's the opposite of paying —"

"I have a job to do in Norkid," Togo's voice dropped dangerously low. "You two can help me accomplish it, if you wish to repay the debt."

TWO

ANOTHER WEEK PASSED AT sea. Maude told her stories, the crew welcomed us as part of their own, and I was able to share the Letters with a few men that accepted Creator as their savior.

Those were the good parts of the travels.

The bad parts were abundant, but I didn't like thinking of them.

However, when one was basically trapped on a ship with the bad things engulfing them, it was hard to ignore it all.

The first predicament was Togo's wish. I hadn't rebuked his request that night, but I had said that we would have to ask Maude for her decision closer to the day we arrived in Norkid. The answer was a pathetic one, but Togo did not press. Did that mean he expected my loyalty, and he thought I would follow through and aid his mission? Or did Togo think I was a coward, and I wouldn't follow through on my debts?

My gut said the latter.

But I would pay my debt. I had to. I had to stay with Togo, too, and Maude, though I didn't understand why. Of course, the Letters did say to lean on Creator, and not my own understanding, so that was what I would have to do.

Togo worked silently, and I worked, too, but tried to focus on Maude's stories, or the crew's questions as they drilled me about Creator.

The second problem was Berk. I didn't know what I had done to offend the first mate, but he did not like me.

He barked orders at me, even if I was doing nothing wrong. He threatened to make me stay aboard longer to pay off anything I might break — though I broke nothing, and did all my work with great care. In the evenings, he pressured me to drink with the crew, or tried to involve me in their crude discussions.

Of course, I held my ground, and tried not to be an ass about it.

But Berk pushed, and pushed, and pushed, and it was not the pushing of a man interested in seeing what the other was made of, to see if he deserved respect — this was the pushing of a man waiting to break another down and devour him. I didn't understand it, but I was on my guard around Berk, though he wasn't as harsh with the others as he was with me.

And the third issue related to the second. Berk was not harsh with the crew, or with Togo, but he showed a strange interest in Maude. I could not fully understand why his attention toward her angered me. It was not rooted in jealousy. In all honesty, I didn't like the way he looked at her because there was something malicious and vile in his gaze, and the fact that anyone dared to look upon any person with such eyes infuriated me.

Wickedness surrounded me. It budded and grew and raged in even the kindest of people. It took root in the heart of man and guided every movement. I knew that Berk was not necessarily evil — and he had shown us goodness — but there was, still, no excuse for a man to look at a woman in such a way, and I wouldn't relax my guard.

Maude had been through enough. She hadn't spoken of her situation before. I didn't know if the master had abused her or assaulted her, or how she felt now, after killing a man — she didn't bring any of it up, and I didn't ask, but I tried to support her in any way I could. And one way in which friends supported one another was by protecting them from people that potentially willed them harm.

I didn't bring up my concerns with Togo. I didn't alert Maude to watch her back. Instead, I worked, and kept as close to Maude as I could — respectfully, of course — while paying attention to Berk's routine.

That night, Berk watched Maude eat on the deck. She ate alone, practically perched on the steps so she was out of the crew's way, but she could still watch the waters. Every so often, she would spot some fish or creature, and laugh and watch like a gleeful child.

Tonight, however, she ate very little, and leaned against the railing as if for support.

As usual, Berk went over after she finished eating, though she hadn't eaten much. He spoke quietly with her for a moment. Then he went below deck.

Maude dropped her head, and from my spot with the crew on the deck, I knew something was wrong. Her hands shook. It was not cold enough to cause her to shake like that. Was it?

I got up and went over to her, sitting beside her. "Maude? Do you feel well?"

"Why do you ask me that?" Maude didn't lift her head. I couldn't see her face. Her shoulders bunched up and she held the bowl of stew with shaky hands.

"You look upset —"

"That's not what you asked. You didn't ask if I was upset. You asked if I was well." Maude's tone tightened. "Do I look ill to you, Bjorn?"

I frowned slightly. "I'm not sure I understand. I'm sorry. I didn't mean to —"

"I am, you know." Maude didn't lift her head. Her hair, fallen from its bun, tangled about her face.

"What?" I leaned closer a bit, trying to hear her better. "I'm sorry —"

"I am ill. But you noticed already, didn't you? Is that why you've taken pity on me? Because I'm weak and —" Maude stopped herself.

"I don't think you're weak," I said. "But I don't understand… You're sick? I can get medicine from the infirmary aboard —"

"It's not that sort of sickness," Maude said. She gripped the bowl of uneaten stew a bit tighter. "It doesn't matter. It changes nothing and you won't believe me."

I scooted closer so I could speak more quietly. "Of course, I'll believe you. And anything you say matters to me. Can I help?" Whatever troubled her, I wanted to fix it for her.

Maude didn't look up. "No one believes me when I say I am sick. Because it is not the type of sick people are accustomed to. Besides, it doesn't matter. It —"

"Could you explain your sickness to me?" I asked. "Are you in pain? Can I get medicine for it?"

Maude lifted her head, finally. Her eyes were red, as if she'd been crying, and she blinked a few times in surprise. Then she said, "No. No, medicine doesn't help."

"What is it, then?" I pressed. "Whatever it is, I want to help." I meant it. It was my duty to help as a priest, but Maude was my friend, too. I hated to see her cry. And I hated knowing Berk had been the one to push her to this desolate place.

Maude dropped her gaze again, shifting uncomfortably. "The healer said it's a sickness she doesn't understand. It's not seen. It's not demonic, exactly — perhaps it is, but no exorcism has helped, and I pray daily for deliverance, but I'm still ill..." She trailed off, tears gleaming in her eyes again. "Regardless of the cause, I'm sick. Tired and weak. I look strong, and I'm grateful my body does work, mind you, I'm not complaining, but it hurts, often, like there's a deep pain, an itch, or aches, and nothing soothes it."

Worry grew in my gut. I studied her pale face, trying to find some sort of idea of how to help — but her defeated posture and tone made it clear that if there had been any resolution to the sickness, she would have found it by now. Still, I couldn't sit by and do nothing.

"There must be something we can do," I said. "If you are in pain, I'll try to find a solution — and I don't think any exorcism will be needed." I kept my voice firm but as positive as possible. Her forlorn spirit didn't need anyone else condemning it.

Maude wiped her eyes roughly. "You're a priest — don't you think I'm possessed? Doesn't the Letters say that by our faith we'll be healed? I-I have faith, Bjorn, and yet..."

And yet, she hurt.

In that moment, fury sparked in me. How many followers of Creator had berated Maude for her pain? How many had claimed she did not love Creator enough? How many had said if she had more faith in His healing kindness, that she would be without sickness?

"I do not think any man is capable of fully understanding Creator's love," I said slowly. "It is written of Creator's divine healing, but I don't think that is all there is to the universe."

Maude winced and looked over. "But —"

"Because there are other stories, and parables, where Creator did not heal every inflicted soul," I continued. "Who are we to say that one is without faith merely because their body or mind is suffering? Creator may let us stumble into rapid waters, but He will not let us drown there. I think we expect Him to take us out of the waters, as well, but it is not always so, and the journey that Creator guides us on is not intended to be burdens... I think they're supposed to be stepping stones to draw us closer to Him... And His love that we struggle to comprehend." I looked down, frowning. "I'm sorry, I'm preaching — you did not ask for a sermon —"

"You don't think I'm a lunatic?" Maude's voice barely came over the cool breeze that whistled overhead through the sails.

I shook my head. "Of course not. You are a follower of Creator. Of course, our lives will be difficult. But you share His love, and the stories, like a true servant. If your body is in pain, or weak, I can't help but think it is merely the darkness trying to keep you from the kingdom's glory.

I don't think it's Creator punishing you or you lacking faith. That's not what I have seen at all." I shrugged.

Tears rolled down Maude's freckled cheeks. She took a slow breath. Had I said something wrong? I wanted my words to help her — they were genuine, and sometimes, I knew, genuine words of love could heal more scars than anything else.

"Thank you, Bjorn," Maude said quietly.

I hesitated for a long moment. "I've noticed Berk speaks with you a lot. You always seem quite upset after he does. May I ask what he is saying?"

Maude wiped her eyes and face. "It's nothing."

I bristled, knowing that it was a lie, but I did not push.

After another moment, Maude whispered, "What do you think it means to live, Bjorn?"

The question hung in the salty air. I let it dwell there for a moment before wrestling it into my mind.

"I suppose it means to love Creator," I said. "However that might look."

"I've given it a lot of thought, since I fell ill," she said softly, staring at her calloused hands. "I think I finally understand it."

She hadn't opened up this much before — not like this, and I felt inadequate, suddenly, because she had openly chosen to trust me with her heart and I was afraid I might fail her.

"What is it?" I asked quietly.

"We can choose to live measly and die peacefully. Or we can choose to live, live, live, and not care about how the end might appear, so long as we know we lived justly." Maude looked up. Her teary eyes slowly glinted with light. "I think to love Creator means to embrace that sort of life, even through pain, trials, or confusion... Do you think I have it right?"

I smiled, looking over the dark depths beyond the ship. "Aye, Maude. I do."

We fell silent again for a moment. Her words sank into my spirit. I would try to cling to them, but I didn't know if I could ever amount to such a life.

But Maude would.

Then, I said, so only she could hear, "Please, from now on, do not hide your pain from me. We are friends, and if I can help you carry your trials, I gladly shall. That's written in the Letters, too."

Maude nodded and sat a bit straighter. "Aye. Thank you. And... well, if I can help you, too, please let me."

I thought of Togo's request — would Maude and I have to help him murder people? I didn't think it best to bring that up right now, so I said, "Of course. Good night, Maude."

Maude went below deck, and I went to find Togo.

THREE

"I HAVE A BAD feeling about Berk," I whispered. Togo was in the bunkroom, sharpening one of his katanas. His long black hair was tied up like usual, but he wore only his black pants, even despite the chill in the air. I stood close by, trying to hide how on edge I was.

Togo shrugged and kept sharpening the blade.

"He keeps talking with Maude."

"A lot of men are talking with Maude."

"This is different."

"It's not. It's a ship full of men. They all want the same thing from Maude." Togo studied the blade carefully before continuing his slow work.

I scowled. "Maybe, but Maude is only disheartened after Berk speaks to her. I have reason to believe he's possibly after something different than just a night of pleasure."

Togo didn't respond. He didn't look up. I huffed, crossing my arms. "Togo! Are you listening to me?"

"What are we supposed to do aboard a ship? He's the first mate. Ignore it."

"But Maude is upset," I argued.

"Women are always upset."

I pinched the bridge of my nose. "We've been over this. The three of us are partners, right? You need our help, and we're repaying a debt. Well, if we don't protect Maude —"

"You are protecting her from nothing. Berk will not touch her." Togo rolled his eyes.

"Maybe I'm not worried about him touching her now," I hissed.

Togo eyed me. "What's the problem?"

"She... she seems broken every time he speaks with her. I am worried he's requesting something of her..."

"Sex?"

"No. Something else."

"Well, speak up, or go to bed." Togo finished sharpening his blade.

"What if Berk knows that she was sold? I mean, it's pretty evident that is what happened, of course, but what if Berk wants to sell her back to the masters? He could take her when we dock and ship her right back and —"

"You have a head full of imagination," Togo said, cutting me off. "If they were going to return Maude to the village, they would not have taken us this far. They would have turned her in at the docks."

"Maybe so." I rubbed the back of my neck. I knew Togo was correct, but I still had a bad feeling in my gut, and it could not be put into words, and I was angry at myself for being unable to voice my concerns, and I couldn't just say what I thought because Togo would not view it as proof and would laugh at me. Well, maybe not laugh. I didn't think the man was capable of laughter or smiling or any sort of sign that he felt human emotion.

Togo sheathed the katana and put the blades against the wall beside him. "You are worried for no reason."

"My gut says otherwise. And I've learned that my gut feelings are usually Creator trying to tell me something. I've learned to follow my gut." I gritted my teeth.

Togo looked up at me without a word. Finally, after a long minute of silence, he said, "We have no evidence Berk is a trader. If there was the slightest hint he has sold people before, I would have been able to tell by now."

"I trust your instinct," I said, "but I still have a bad feeling."

"Do you think he wants to keep Maude for himself?" Togo asked. "She's clearly not afraid of being at sea, and she is beautiful. He might be lonely."

"Possibly." I nodded. "Maude didn't say, but his tenacity is steadfast, and that speaks volumes."

"If he is interested in her, why don't you leave it alone? He has money. Women like that." Togo frowned.

"Togo!" I growled.

"Do you want her?"

"No. We're partners — aren't you concerned over her wellbeing?"

"No."

I groaned. "Well, I am. She's a sister in Creator, and I don't want to watch her cry every time some first mate speaks to her!"

Togo hesitated at that, and looked across the bunkroom. "She cries?"

The question was so quiet, and asked with genuine confusion. It caught me off guard. "Yes," I said. "She did. She won't tell me what he says... but I am worried."

"We have no idea why you are worried, and no proof Berk has done anything to harm her. Thus, we do nothing. For now." Togo rolled over in his hammock.

For now. His two words left me with a sliver of hope that maybe, possibly, Togo would help me keep Maude safe. Of course, he might change his mind: he didn't even want us as partners, after all. But he hadn't killed us yet, and I thought we truly had a mutual understanding at this point. His concern — I viewed it as concern, anyway — toward Maude gave me hope he had a soul left, even if he didn't act on it often, as a mercenary greatly feared by many.

I cleaned up, climbed into my hammock without falling out this time, and slept restlessly all night.

I dreamed about the men and women in the streets of Norkid.

I dreamed about the cold alleys. The frigid snow falling all around, making my feet and hands ache, making the world feel big and empty.

I dreamed about the blood dripping into the piles of white snow.

I dreamed about hands, big hands, strong hands, wrapping around my neck.

I dreamed about it all again and again, like I had since I was a child, until I woke early in the morning.

FOUR

On the third week of travel, we arrived at Port Hunya.

The cool morning breeze rippled across the ship. The crew worked to prepare to anchor, most of them whistling and singing a sea shanty I hadn't heard before. Maude sang with them too, and it was most amusing to hear a small woman sing about such manly things.

I kept close to Maude. She perched on the deck, watching the land grow closer, and eventually, her singing stopped. A strange silence came over her.

I took a brief break from my duties and went over. "Maude?"

"Hm?" She immediately looked up with a smile, albeit a false one.

"You're in pain now?" I asked. It felt like intruding, but I genuinely wanted to know.

Maude's smile faltered. "Aye." She glanced back toward Port Hunya. "We're almost there," she said wistfully, sighing. "I wonder how long it'll take us to fulfill our debt to Togo and then return home."

"Oh." I cringed inside. I didn't like how she changed the subject so quickly, but if she did not want to talk about her pain, I would respect that. "Well, probably not very long."

"He's a legend," her voice dropped, "we'll probably be in his debt forever."

I gulped and shook my head. "Not at all! He's not as monstrous as that."

"You know him well?"

The question took me back. I had told Maude my story of meeting Togo, so of course, she knew I didn't know the man much more than she did. "Well... No." I rubbed sweat and grime from my forehead. Briefly, I told her of how Togo and I had met.

She smiled a bit and looked down at the deep still waters below the *Sinner*. "It is a miracle he found you in time, hm?"

"Aye." I laughed. "And… anyway, while I haven't known him much longer than I've known you, I just have a good idea of people's intentions, is all."

"Discernment is a good gift," Maude said.

"It can be." It also caused great pain and heartache, but Maude probably already knew that.

"Well, if you trust him, I do, too. We'll repay our debts and be off again in no time." Maude flashed a smile again — it was a bit less fake. "Do you know what he'll need from us as payback?"

"Uh, I'm sure he'll mention it when we dock." I glanced toward the helm of the ship, feeling eyes on my back. Sure enough, Berk watched us, his arms crossed, his gaze sharp enough to skin a cow alive.

Maude dropped her head again. "I'm sorry—"

"Apologize for nothing," I mumbled, "the man has been on my back since we boarded the ship."

"I —" Maude began to speak, but stopped herself, and anger rose in my chest. Had she been close to telling me what she thought of him? Of what he had been saying to her?

"We're almost free," I said firmly. "Just hang on a bit longer. Rest here."

I hurried back to work alongside Togo.

When the ship anchored, a few of the crewmates went to shore, along with Togo, Maude, and I. The captain and Berk led us into the port.

Port Hunya was a grand, luxurious port, with many shops, inns, saloons, homes, smithies, and other trading posts. People wove in and out of the stores, and wagons and horses hurried along the cobblestone streets. It was cool here — cooler than it had been in the east. Immediately, the chill in the air bit into my skin, and I cast a worried glance at Maude.

Maude walked silently, her head down, between me and Togo, as if we could provide some fortress of protection against the bustling city. I wondered if this was the port where she had been shipped from — was she struggling with fear? Did she remember the terror of being sold and trafficked?

Rage kindled in my chest. I could not undo Maude's past, but I could protect her now. I leaned over a bit, quickly whispering, "Stay close, Maude. Everything is all right. You're safe with us." I straightened and kept walking, so she didn't feel pressured.

Maude didn't speak a word, but I practically felt her tense body relax slightly at my side. However, my gaze caught Berk's, who led the group. He looked ahead again, saying, "Why don't we all get a bite to eat at Lucky Cat's?"

The crewmates agreed hastily. Togo frowned, and I didn't like the display of emotion. I glanced at Maude, but before I could say anything, the group herded us toward the closest saloon. It was large, and packed full of gruff men, and men smoked on the deck.

On the wooden deck of the saloon, Berk took Maude by the arm, and I immediately got between them. "Maude and I should go get some rooms reserved at the inn—"

"There are rooms above the saloon," Berk replied. He didn't try to grab Maude again since she kept behind me — and Togo.

Frustrated, I said, "It's too loud here." I glanced at the doors. Already, the ruckus of the saloon wafted into the streets. Men's voices rattled with cheers and music. The smell of booze made my nose itch. "Besides, it's no place for a lady."

Berk tilted his head, but before he could speak, the captain laughed. "Come along, come along! We'll not let a soul harm Miss Maude! But this is the best food you'll ever taste, and they're the only place around that'll give us discounts on the prices!"

With that, the crew hurried inside, and Maude slowly stepped toward the door.

I didn't want to make a scene — especially since Maude took the step forward. If she was willing to go along with things, I'd do the same, if only to keep a watch over her.

Togo led our trio alongside the crew. Right away, the bartender at the counter called out to the captain. "I had hoped the sea had gotcha! What can I get for your damned ass?"

The captain quipped back, and the crew ordered rounds of drinks and large portions of meals. Captain ordered three meals for us, too, and slapped my back with a grin. "It's on us! You three have pulled your weight. Enjoy!"

Berk's frown darkened as he stepped over and sat beside Captain. The crew sat in booths against the far left wall, but the captain dragged the three of us beside him, so we cramped into the booth. Maude sat smashed between Togo and I.

"Thirsty? Whaddya drink?" Captain asked Togo, then called to the bartender, "Some mead for the priest, will ya, Charles? He doesn't drink!"

I gulped. "Um, could I get water?"

"And one whiskey," Togo added.

Captain glanced at Maude. "What'll Miss Maude like?"

"Um —"

"Mead," Berk said.

I scowled, but Maude spoke up. "Tea, please."

"Tea?" Captain sighed and called to the bartender. "Your finest tea, for the miss!"

In minutes, we all had our drinks, and I nursed my water quietly as the captain laughed and chatted with his crew and some strangers that approached the table.

Clearly, the crew had a good reputation around here — but despite the merry atmosphere, Berk's scowl never left his face. He cast me the occasional glare. I didn't speak. I didn't want to cause problems — but I also wasn't going to stand down if he decided to pull anything foolish.

When the food was served — Togo, Maude, and I were given heaping servings of stew, vegetables, bread, and butter — the crew almost went quiet, too busy shoving food into their mouths to talk.

Berk, however, picked at his food and eyed Maude. "Enjoying the meal?" he asked.

"Aye. Thank you." Maude glanced at the captain. She ate heartily.

The captain beamed and slapped my back again. "See? I told you the food was worth the noise!"

"You *are* the noise!" the bartender called over.

"Stay out of private conversations!" Captain jested back, shoveling food into his mouth.

Berk leaned forward. "You know, Maude, we were looking for another member of the crew, just recently, actually."

The captain whined. "Must we talk about work now? Ease up, Berk! Take a day off!" He kept eating, but Berk smiled, merely pacifying his friend's complaints.

"We would appreciate help with the management of the tradings — someone to help us calculate costs, orders, and the like." Berk continued.

Maude forced more food into her mouth. She didn't answer.

"The pay is good," Berk said firmly.

Captain laughed and winked at Maude. "The pay would be even better for a lovely lady like you!"

As terrible as it sounded, Captain's flirting didn't bother me much — I knew he respected Maude, and I couldn't imagine him posing any threat to her. And if Maude ever told him that she was not interested in his pursuit, I believed the man would respect her wishes and cease. But Berk was a different story. My gut told me that he was no good, even if I had no proof, like Togo wanted.

Maude cleared her throat, straightening a bit as she met Captain's gaze. "I appreciate the offer, really, but —"

"Your illness would not prohibit you from earning the wage," Berk said, tone icy.

I bristled and almost came out of my seat. How did he know about Maude's sickness? He spoke the words with such apathy — it enraged me. Was he trying to coerce Maude into what he wanted by using her sickness as a weakness against her?

Maude paled, head dropping. She didn't argue.

Before I could speak, Togo set his whiskey down. "Maude already has a job."

Maude and I lifted our heads at him in surprise.

"Oh?" Berk asked, raising one eyebrow. "That's not what she told me."

"Perhaps because she has enough sense to maintain a private life," Togo replied. Head tilting, he smiled at Berk.

I had never seen such a dangerous smile before.

"Maude and Bjorn work for me," Togo said.

That settled the matter. Berk finished his mead and ordered another round, though Captain beamed. "Aha! That's it, then! You said they were clients but they're employees! That makes much more sense — though I'd never assumed the legend needed aid?"

"Grunt work," Togo said with a wink.

Captain scoffed. "You'll bite the dust one day, Togo the Black Angel! And you two! Don't get caught in the crossfires!" He waved at Maude and I, his words already beginning to slur. The captain was a surprisingly lightweight drinker, but he got another round eagerly.

Togo's smile remained cold as ice on his face. I grimaced, changing the subject to discuss something else besides Togo or Maude.

FIVE

AFTER A FEW HOURS of eating and drinking, the crew slowly dispersed. A few men went upstairs with some harlots. A few other crewmates went upstairs to go to sleep.

Maude finished her meal and her eyelids drooped, but she listened to the captain tell a drunken tale. He rambled on about how they had once ran into some great sea monster. Togo finished his whiskey, glancing at me with a small frown.

I took the look as it was time to retire. I cleared my throat. "Thank you for the dinner, Captain. I think we'd best get to bed now, but thank you for the story, too."

Captain sighed and waved us on, downing the rest of his mead. "Fine, fine! We'll finish this tale another night!"

"Aye, of course." I smiled and stood. Maude and Togo followed in my steps, but Berk stood, too, and got close to Maude.

"I'll lead you to your room, Maude," Berk said. "It's on my floor. Togo and Bjorn have the room above us."

I tensed. They had already arranged our rooms? When had they gotten the chance to do so? Or were rooming arrangements already set because the captain had business with the keeper?

"There's no need," I said quickly.

"They sleep in my quarters," Togo added, stepping forward. He tilted his head at Berk, a silent warning in his dark eyes. Of course, he was not someone any of the others would want to anger — and Berk stepped down again.

"Fine," Berk said, "as you wish, Black Angel."

The captain told us where to find our room. Togo nodded once.

Fighting my anger, I smiled at the captain, who drank obviously, and then led Maude after Togo.

Our room was on the third floor. Togo had our packs, and I opened the room door quickly. Togo stepped in and set the packs on the small, rickety wooden table to the left of the room. The room had two beds, small ones, but they looked clean. A small wash basin sat to the side beside the hearth, and a wooden chair stood against the wall beside the small, curtained window that overlooked the alley below.

I locked the door behind us. "I'm sorry about this, Maude," I said.

"I'd rather sleep here than alone." Maude shrugged weakly.

"There's a washroom downstairs. Grab your things and we'll go clean up." Togo opened the packs.

We gathered clean clothes, then went back downstairs. We avoided the dining hall, and made our way to the bathing house outside, where we bathed — Maude washed in the women's quarters, of course, but I stood guard outside to ensure no one bothered her — and then returned to our room, clean again.

I started a fire in the hearth, and Togo put our packs away before he grabbed his pipe, filled it, and lit it. He sat on the wooden chair.

Maude sat on the edge of one of the beds, watching me, her hands in her lap moving, fidgeting, folding, wringing. I glanced up as the fire settled and crackled. "Maude?"

"He wasn't supposed to know," Maude said quickly. "About me being sick. I didn't say anything — he found me one night — he wasn't supposed to say anything."

"He has no power or control over you," I said. "Please, don't worry." The very idea of Maude being in pain, and being discovered and targeted by Berk, sparked rage, but I couldn't act on it now.

Maude glanced at Togo. Her pale face darkened, and her hands turned to fists. "Togo — I can still return my debt. I'm not weak or helpless. Please, let me prove it."

Togo puffed smoke, finally looking our way with a quirked brow. "You have nothing to prove to me."

"But I'm... I'm weak. Sick. Physically —"

"Perhaps," Togo said, cutting her off, "but even so, you remain with us, and after all, you killed a village chief to survive. Your body may be different than most, but it is not less deserving of life or freedom."

I gulped — I hadn't expected Togo to believe in sanctity of life, but I added, "Yes, Togo's right."

Maude dropped her head. Was she going to cry? I didn't want that. But before I could stand and try to comfort her, Maude straightened her shoulders again and eyed Togo. "So, what's our duty to repay you?"

Togo huffed more smoke and watched it waft through the dim room, pierced only by the large, growing fire in the hearth. "We'll discuss it in the morning."

My gut twisted, but I nodded once and sat on the other bed. Maude curled up in her bed, vanishing under the covers.

I sprawled out on the other bed until Togo came over, and then I got on my side, and he laid down silently. I didn't toss and turn, and fell asleep eventually.

I dreamed of the big hands, the crimson snow, the dark alley, and crying and pain.

I woke with a jerk. My right arm swung out. It slammed into something hard, but a hand grabbed my forearm midair.

Panic washed over me like cold water. I twisted my neck, tensing.

Togo released my arm. The fire burning in the hearth cast shadows over his face. He said nothing.

I pulled my arm back quickly, heart hammering in my throat. "Sorry," I whispered. Togo didn't answer. Was he angry? Had I hit him, or had he caught my arm before it got close? Had he even been asleep?

Togo returned to looking at the ceiling in the darkness. I gulped and rolled over, putting my back to him. I didn't like showing weakness in front of Togo, but it didn't matter, exactly. We still had a mission to do, and he had not left us yet, so he probably wouldn't.

I would prove to Togo that I could repay my debt. I would prove to Togo that a man of Creator could still be brave and strong. I would prove to Togo that his spirit could be saved, too. Somehow, I'd do that by walking the thin line between the dark and the light.

And if I could do that — if I could save Togo and Maude, no matter what insane mission I had to follow — then maybe my soul could find salvation, too. I knew the

Letters spoke that faith was not created through works. But my heart — my bloody hands — could not believe it.

And so I fought, and I fought, and I fought, for a reason, a purpose; the right to live.

SIX

EARLY IN THE MORNING, in the smoky streets of Port Hunya, our trio bid goodbye to the crew of *Sinner*. Captain slapped Togo and I on the back briskly, and kissed Maude's hand, telling us how grateful he had been for our help, and what a pleasure it had been to have a famous storyteller aboard. Maude blushed, but thanked him for the flattery.

I grinned. "She won't forget you when she's a legendary storyteller across all the territories."

Captain laughed and nodded, and Maude smiled a bit wider. It was good to see her smile.

Berk eyed Togo, stepping forward and offering a hand. "I hope to see you all again," Berk said firmly.

It sounded like a threat.

"One day," Togo said with a sly smile. He shook Berk's hand before stepping to the side. "We'd best be off. The horses are waiting." Togo had already purchased three fine mares before the sun rose. They stood hitched to the post near the saloon's exit.

Maude nodded. "Thank you," she told the captain quickly, and followed Togo over to the mares.

I took a breath of the cool, crisp morning air, and shook the captain's hand. "Thank you. Truly."

"Anytime, priest man," Captain said with a grin. "Pleasure meeting you and hearing about your God. I might have to give him a prayer one of these days."

I flashed a smile. "He's always listening." I left the crew behind and followed after my motley-looking friends. We mounted our mares and began our journey toward Norkid.

SEVEN

We left Port Hunya far behind on our first day of travel. Togo took an unbeaten path, far from the main roads that civilians traveled to and fro, but we didn't argue.

The horses trodded, and we stopped them occasionally so they could rest or drink at the streams we found along the journey. It was evident Togo knew this land as well as he had the eastern land. This irked me. Togo was a legend — but seeing his steadfast skills in action grew unnerving. Of course, he wasn't my enemy. And he had not left us, so our debts were still to be paid, and we were, until Togo abandoned us, a trio.

And until Togo left, or one of us died, I would remain at his side to fulfill my duty to Creator.

Would this duty be to help lead him to Creator's love and light?

Or would it be some other duty? Whatever it was, I was ready and willing.

And as we traveled, I prayed. I prayed for Maude, and for Creator to heal her, if it was His will, and then I prayed that if it was not His will to heal Maude's aching body, that He would give her courage and peace to face her path that He had set before her.

I prayed for Togo, too, and that the Creator would soften his heart — and lead him toward the light.

My prayers were cut short as Maude's mare slowed until it was behind us. Togo didn't slow down, but I did, shifting in the leather saddle. "Maude?" I glanced back at her. "Is everything all right?"

Maude's pale face twisted slightly, and she looked about at the rolling fields of grass and tall, dense trees. "No."

"What is it?" I stopped my mare. The cool breeze nipped my cheeks and ruffled my hair and beard. "Should we take a break?" If she was in pain, I didn't want her pushing herself too much.

"Something's wrong," Maude said weakly. Her gaze settled on the thick trees ahead of us. The trail we took was old and unmarked. Surely, no one would be along it. I had never known it to even exist until Togo started us along it. The woods were dense and overgrown with plenty of dead, dry brush.

What could be wrong?

Still, I trusted Maude's instinct. I reined my horse beside Maude's. "What is?"

Togo kept his mare steady, not looking back or slowing down as he said, "Keep moving."

I trusted Togo's instinct, too, and since we both intended to keep Maude safe—well, Togo had not said forthright that was his mission or goal, but he had stood up for Maude in the tavern, when she had been uncomfortable and upset, and I didn't imagine a man would do such a thing if he did not care for the woman—I followed Togo's lead.

I started my mare forward but reached out and gently coaxed Maude's mare along, too. The mare, sensing Maude's sudden unease, hesitated, but followed. Maude leaned forward a little, sweat beading at her temples.

Something was wrong — but with Maude.

"Maude?" I frowned. "What's —"

Thwink.

Something hit the tree just beyond us, right at our head level. I glanced up and gaped at the arrow piercing the dark tree. Had that been there before? No, that was new.

Another arrow whizzed past my ear, and I immediately urged our mares onward. Maude clutched her saddle horn, leaning forward till her face almost vanished in the mare's thick mane as we fled down the path.

Togo jumped off his mare's back at the path's turn, tumbling and rolling into the thick brush to our left. I gasped, but before I could call out to see if he was all right, Maude pitched forward, too. She dumped off the horse and dropped into the bushes to our right.

I jerked my horse to a stop, panic rising. "Maude!" She was already sick — as if having some sort of episode. What if she had gotten trampled after she fell? Or hit a rock?

More arrows flew over my head and I dismounted hastily.

I was not the man I used to be — but I was a fool, and a fool rushes into danger without care for his own soul, if it means possibly protecting another's.

So I tumbled into the brush.

Maude lay in the leaves and mud, and I didn't see blood, but I didn't slow down to really look. I tackled her, covering her body with my own as more arrows hit the trees and ground nearby. One nicked my arm, but I clutched Maude tightly in the dirt.

I had no weapon. I could find a rock or stick, but even then, whoever hunted us wielded arrows, and they would kill me before I got close. Still, I couldn't count on Togo to protect us now.

I lifted my head a bit, searching desperately for some sort of weapon as I breathed a prayer. "Creator, protect us."

Dirt and leaves surrounded me. Not a rock or large stick in sight.

How was that possible? And at such a time as this? It felt cruelly ironic.

Another arrow hit the ground right beside my hand, and I craned my neck to see the attackers. At the top of the small ditch we had fallen in, three men stood, their bows drawn and arrows nocked. The tallest man, with a white bandana around his face, called, "Be still! We'll only take the girl!"

They wanted Maude? Bristling, I didn't get up from shielding Maude with my body. "I'm not sure I understand!" I called back, hoping I could play dumb.

"Release the woman!" the second man snapped, waving his bow a bit as if that would shut me up. "Now!"

How could they be after Maude? Who were they? There was no way that the village in the east had somehow sent reinforcements here. But then, who else would be after Maude? Had Berk hired mercenaries to retain her? Had he been that jealous and haughty?

"Why?" I yelled. Maude remained unconscious beneath me. Sweat poured down her face, and her breathing was steady but ragged, as if it pained her. I had no idea what was happening with her, but I wouldn't let anyone take her. She was free — and I would protect her freedom with my last breath.

"Release her!" the tall man ordered. Before the three men could come down the ditch, or shoot me in my thick skull, a flash of black appeared.

As fast as it came, the black flash was gone. The three men dropped to the ground — their corpses bleeding profusely on the leaves and sinking into the mud puddle they fell in.

Togo stepped down the ditch, his bloody katanas in hand. He didn't look at the bodies. He didn't show remorse or relief.

The Black Angel had saved us.

And I hated myself for it.

It was my fault the man shed more blood — how could I lead his soul to Creator if I was the reason his soul continued to be damned?

Perhaps I viewed it incorrectly. But as I watched Togo approach, with eyes like ice and blood dripping from his blades, I wondered if I could truly save him, like I hoped Creator intended.

Maybe I truly wasn't strong enough to do so. Maybe the Black Angel was too much for me.

"Do you hear me?" Togo asked, tone sharp. He stood over me in the dirt. "Stand."

I blinked once. Then glanced down at Maude, panic swelling. I had zoned out. Why had I done that in the heat of the moment now? "She's sick," I said hastily.

"She is not as sick as you think," Togo said, wiping the blood off his katanas with a shirt he had taken from one of the corpses. When had he grabbed that? A moment ago, when I had been lost in panicked thoughts?

"What?"

"Maude does have illnesses of the body," Togo continued, "but what we witnessed now was a reaction to her spirit being foretold of danger — a physical toll occurs, but she is not sick, in the essence we view physical sickness."

"But she's already ill, this sort of toll cannot be good for her!" I argued.

"True, it isn't," Togo agreed, sheathing his katanas. He tilted his head at me. "Gather her. I'll fetch the horses."

Mind spinning, I checked Maude's pulse — it was strong, along with her breathing — and scooped her up. I carried her up the ditch. Togo brought the horses over after a moment of searching. I mounted, and he helped put Maude in front of me so I could hold her there, and then Togo ponied the third mare to his own. He mounted, and we set off again, leaving the bodies and blood behind us.

I prayed for the three men's souls.

And I prayed for forgiveness for myself, too.

MAUDE DID NOT WAKE. After over an hour of travel, I finally summoned my wits about me. "Togo?" I asked, voice heavy.

Togo kept his gaze on the path ahead. The sun dwindled now, and we would make camp soon.

"Those men were after Maude," I said.

"Aye."

"And... and it would not be because of the village chief sending after her, of course, that's not possible. And it's unlikely Berk sent anyone after her." I trailed off.

Togo did not argue.

"So, who was after her?" I whispered.

Togo did not answer.

"Why would anyone be after Maude? She told us of her homeland — she's not a princess, or a noblewoman, or a lady. She's not a peasant, or some homeless gypsy, but she's not rich — so why would anyone need her? And she's not Gifted." I glanced down at Maude's pale face. She remained slumped against me as we rode.

Togo still said nothing.

I took a slow breath. "You did not seem surprised that we were hunted," I said. "Nor did you seem shocked to discover Berk's interest... But you protected Maude from Berk. So I must believe you care for her, even if you do not care for me, and thus, we share the common goal of at least wanting Maude safe — but if there is a danger here that I am unaware of, but you know, please do not leave me arrogant, Togo." I watched him, tone firm, hiding my desperation the best I could.

Togo rode in silence for another minute, then he drew his horse alongside mine. He shifted the reins in his hands, speaking simply. "Maude is Gifted."

"What? No, she isn't. Gifted wield actual Gifts — like fire, or water, or they heal, or... You know, things like that. Gifts are from Creator, but they're tangible things." I frowned in confusion.

"Some." He nodded. "But not every Gift is tangible. Not every Gift is boisterous."

I furrowed my brows, studying him. The man did not believe in Creator, but still, it was not uncommon for anyone to have a brief understanding of the Gifts and how they worked. "Why do you say she is Gifted?"

"Because she can prophesy," Togo said. "That is one of the Gifts, is it not? Only you and your people that follow Creator believe the Gift is long lost, is that true?"

"Most believers do believe those... ancient Gifts are lost, but I do not believe such." I shook my head. "But why do you say that about Maude? Did she tell you this?"

"No," Togo said. I winced at him. "Then how did you know this?"

Togo met my gaze and sighed. "I told you. I can sense things about people."

"This is a lot to know," I said. "Does Maude know that you're aware of all of this?"

"No. She has no need to know."

"But —"

"If you tell her I know she is Gifted, she will be more afraid than she already is. I am a mercenary, after all. She would fear me as the enemy, and view her returning my debt as me as enslaving her instead. I do not wish that. Do you?"

Togo's cutting eyes made me swallow hard before answering. "I suppose not." But I added, "You've known this the entire time, then?"

He nodded.

"You didn't say anything to me."

"You said nothing when you discovered she was ill."

I shook my head. "I—"

"You protected her privacy, the same as I."

"Aye. I suppose. But we need to discuss it all with her. We should all be on the same path before we continue forward." I didn't like the feeling that Togo had known so much and said nothing. Being Gifted, especially if the Gift was not tangible as most were nowadays, was no small matter. Of course, Togo hadn't wanted to uncover Maude — but how had he even known? Was his discernment that great? I prayed for mine to be strong — and I had not noticed that. I had failed Maude. If I had known more about what she kept hidden, I could have helped her more by now.

Togo grunted and watched the woods.

"Where are we going, anyway? You told me we would help you with a job in Norkid. What sort of mission is it?" I tried changing the subject.

"Does it matter what sort of mission it is?"

"It does. I know who you are, Togo. I know it cannot be a safe mission. I don't want Maude harmed. But we will repay our debt."

"You think I would endanger a woman?" Togo frowned.

"No. But I wish you would communicate with us."

"You seem to already have an assumption of what sort of job it is. What do you think?" He eyed me out of the corner of his eyes.

I nodded slowly. "I know mercenaries kill and kidnap often."

"We do."

"And Norkid is a land of many rich men. So perhaps you're hunting a nobleman at the discretion of another rich man or politician. Considering your high stature among your kind, I am inclined to believe you are hunting someone very important. A royal, perhaps." I held his gaze, voice steady. Togo didn't look away. His expression didn't reveal if I was correct or not. "But you've also accepted our aid, so it is not a job that's too much work or you would not risk us ruining it."

"So in other words, you think I am going to assassinate the new prince being crowned in Norkid this winter solstice?" Togo asked.

Unnerved by his matter-of-fact question, I said, "Are you?"

"I've had offers to do such."

I shifted in my saddle, pulling Maude a bit closer, but she slept soundly. "It is true, then? You want our help killing Prince Balder?"

The prince was not a bad man, uncorrupted by the local politics that grew worse and harsher with each passing year. Norkid had once been a stronghold of honor and unity. Now, hoodlums roamed every street, and the royals were heavily paid by foreigners or enemies to keep silent and to feed the never-ending machine of evil.

But the prince had promised a new future.

It was no wonder he had a price tag on his head.

"Hmm." Togo shrugged. "I've considered the job. Having partners that know the city better than I would be useful."

"You don't know Norkid?" I blanched.

"Very little. I've only been there once for a mission." Togo sighed. "But you and Maude lived there. It seems fate would have me kill the prince, does it not?"

"I didn't take you as a man to believe in fate," I mustered. Gut clenching, I sought some sort of excuse as to why the mission would be a terrible failure.

Except this was the Black Angel I was now partners with. The legend that failed no mission and left no survivors.

If we went against the prince, he stood no chance.

"When you covered Maude in those bushes," Togo began, jarring me from my sick reveries, "you sought a weapon, and when none was to be found, you were still preparing yourself to fight a losing battle. You have the instincts of a man that has endured and survived danger — but you are a priest, and not a soldier or mercenary."

As Togo spoke, my blood grew colder.

Did he know?

"You fool many," Togo said, voice dropping. He looked over. "But you have not fooled me."

"I've not tried to fool a soul," I said. "I am as I say I am, Togo."

"You are. But a man is many men combined in one tormented soul. That is what it is to be alive: it is to have lived countless lives. The man you are now is not the only man you have been." Togo put his eyes on our path ahead once more. "I do not expect you to slaughter the young prince. I understand that a priest would urge the prince to take over the kingdom, and to restore peace and love, yes? But if you are genuine, you will see how many souls would be lost if the prince did take the throne."

Heart rushing into my throat, I said, "We are not the judges to decide who lives and who dies in that kingdom, Togo."

"You would rather a trafficker, or a politician, or a wizard master make the decision instead?"

"If you kill the prince, the kingdom will continue to rot. How many will continue to die then?"

"And if the prince tries to restore the nation, how many souls will die of hunger, or murder, or battle?"

Sweat beaded at my temples and stuck my palms to my reins. My hammering heart rang in my ears. I wanted to argue — but who was I to?

"We cannot choose, just as they cannot," I said.

"Someone always decides fate. It is a fool's belief to think that by remaining peaceful, the outcome will also be peaceful." Togo shrugged, and silence fell between us.

EIGHT

An owl hooked overhead as we set up camp in a small clearing in the forest. I always traveled in the world Creator had built, finding some reason to be grateful. Even though my back ached from sleeping in the dirt so much, my skin was turning brown from the mud as the rain began pouring, and the cool elements made my bones cold as ice... I tried to remind myself that it could be worse.

Of course, Maude had not woken, and I wasn't sure what could be more worse than that tonight.

Togo made quick work — he built a small lean-to out of tree branches, just big enough for us to hunker under with Maude between us. Mud and rain still surrounded us, but the little sanctuary kept us mostly dry. I had made similar lean-tos during my travels, and was always amazed at how strong and water-proof some limbs and branches could be.

I was also amazed at how quickly Togo had built the structure. But I didn't mention that.

"Think it'll let up soon?" I asked Togo quietly.

Togo leaned against our packs. "Probably."

"She hasn't woken..." I began, worry making my stomach twist.

"She just needs sleep."

I held my tongue, and watched the rain pour just feet away from me. It slammed into the dirt, causing mud to race along and the bushes to lean and sway. Thunder rolled as darkness settled over the forest, and the storm wept.

It sounded a lot like how my spirit felt.

THE RAIN SLOWED DURING the night. It pattered against the ground until it stopped, leaving a peaceful silence over the forest. Togo sighed and straightened. "I'll start a fire if I can find some dry wood." He crawled out from the small lean-to without another word, vanishing into the woods.

I eased Maude against the packs, so she was as dry as could be, and comfortable, and put one of the blankets over her carefully. Then I searched for some dry kindling, to no avail, until Togo returned with dry kindling and some dead branches.

Silent, Togo set to work starting the fire. I pulled some rations from the packs, trying not to wake Maude. I wanted her to wake, to eat, but she slept as if dead. She did need it, that much was clear, but it still worried me.

I knelt beside the fire with Togo. It fought hard to breathe, and Togo blew on it carefully until the kindling caught flame. The little fire grew, beating back the darkness that engulfed us.

Though I was soaked, with my clothes and hair plastered to my body, and chilled to the bone, and worried sick for Maude, and terrified I might lose Togo's soul (of course, was it mine to lose?) — the little flame in the cold, wet forest gave me hope. It was a beacon: a reminder that no matter what I faced, I couldn't stop. I couldn't allow my heart to grow weary, even now, when I had no idea what to do next, and it felt like Creator had led me into a mess and left me in it alone.

I shook myself from my reveries. I put the rations in a pot over the fire, and we kept quiet as the food sizzled, then we pulled it off and ate. Togo finished first, and looked across the little clearing toward Maude. "We'll make her coffee when she wakes."

"She doesn't like coffee," I said.

"It'll help her stay awake. She's tired, but the journey is not over yet." Togo eyed me. "You want her returned home safely, yes?"

"Of course," I said tightly. "That's why I began this journey."

"Then she'll need to be alert enough to avoid the enemies chasing her. If her Gift foresees another attack, we'll survive, but it will continue to be a toll on her body." Togo shrugged. "This is her reality. A constant battle between mind and body. It's hell."

Indignation rose in my chest. "Maude's life is not hell. You are not one to speak of such things." Maude was kind, and gentle, and cheerful, and...

And sad. And lonely. And hurting. And afraid.

Creator told His followers to be courageous, and to take heart, and Maude did so: but she wept, and she ached, and bled. That was life: to feel everything, no matter how painful. Every trial, every tear, and drop of blood, brought us closer to being a new being in Creator, right? So, then, if life was nothing but living countless lives as one spirit, did it not mean that the most broken among us were the closest to Creator, and to their real purpose, if our purpose was to live repeatedly for Creator, so that we would grow closer to His love, and eventually move into eternity?

Togo watched the flames. They cast shadows over his face. "I suppose I'm not. But would you want to live a life in constant pain? She has been belittled, berated, shunned, rejected, all because her body is weaker than others. It does not seem much of a life to me."

Face hot with rage, I said sharply, but my tone did not raise, "I don't want to hear those words coming from a mercenary! She has worth — she is a kind soul! Is it so terrible for a soul to be on fire while the body is weak? Is it so cursed? Is it so disappointing?" Breathing ragged, I hissed, "You agreed we would protect her. How could you say this, then? How can you defend Maude from Berk, and from those wild men, and still think such things?"

"Because I do not understand her, or you," Togo said, looking up.

My burst of anger immediately subsided. "What?"

"You both are broken souls — you are human. Yet, you believe in some fairy tales that give you the audacity to keep living, even when neither of you wish to." Togo's words cut me deep, as if a wolf were tossing my heart around in a pool of alcohol.

"I want to live. Maude does, too. Not everyone is miserable with their life," I said. "We have Creator — our lives are saved, and they are purposeful. If you do not understand hope, then you must first understand Creator."

Was I reaching him? At last? After almost months of travel, he had never allowed me any chance to truly discuss Creator with him — and he had certainly never brought it up like this before.

But just as quickly as Togo brought up the subject, did he kill it. "Perhaps. If it helps you both survive this world, who am I to detest it."

We were silent until morning.

NINE

"I'm sorry," Maude woke up breathing those words in a panicked gasp.

I reached over and patted her shoulder. "It's all well, Maude!" I kept my tone cheery. Too cheery. My own voice made me want to stab my eyes out. But I needed to reassure Maude — if her physical state worsened at the detriment of her mental state, I could at least try to ease her mind, and hopefully help her rest, too.

"I've finished you some breakfast. And there's coffee. Some coffee will help give you a boost, yes? We've got traveling left to do. In no time, we'll reach a village, and we'll find another inn. It'll beat sleeping in the rain, for certain," I said, not waiting for Maude to speak.

Maude sat up weakly, blinking between Togo and I. Then she dropped her head, wiping at some dried mud on her arms. "I..."

"It's all right. Please, eat something first. Then we can talk," I said. Handing her a plate of warmed jerky, thin bread, and some grilled vegetables, I then poured her a mug of coffee.

Maude sat huddled under the blanket, devouring the food and sipping the coffee.

The sun rose and cast gentle light over the cold, wet forest. I shivered slightly against the growing chill, courtesy of the rain.

"They were after me," Maude said after a while, her voice hanging in the chilly, damp morning air.

I cringed. Would she tell us about her Gift now?

It was strange — I was not angry or hurt that Maude had not told me about the Gift. Instead, I wanted to protect her even more. Maybe she had not told me the truth because she feared I might be some enemy against her. Or maybe she had not told me the truth because she had wanted to protect me. No matter her reason, I still was her friend, and still would defend her.

And, at this rate, Togo seemed to be on that same path, too.

But would Maude be truthful now? Why? Had the fiasco pushed her to her mental limits, and she couldn't hide any longer? I gulped, pain tightening my chest.

In the cool morning, under the chill of the dew, as the fire danced, Maude met our gazes briefly.

"I'm Gifted," Maude said. She picked at some mud on her arm. "I..." She hesitated again. Her eyes were heavy, her face pale as death, but she mustered, "Creator speaks to me, and when He does, it happens."

"Soothsaying?" Togo said.

"No!" Maude winced. "It is not dark magic."

"Prophesying," I said softly. "As the Letters mentioned."

"S-something like that," Maude said, expression twisting. "Sometimes He tells me of big things, sometimes of little things."

"You saw the hunters coming yesterday?" I asked.

"I did."

"Your response probably saved us," I said.

Maude shook her head. "Togo knew they were there."

"It is unwise to demean your own gifting," Togo said with a frown. Maude dropped her head. "Did you recognize who followed us?"

"No," Maude said.

"More will follow?" Togo asked.

Maude slumped slightly, and I urged her to drink more coffee to warm up. After she got a bit more down, she said, "I don't know that either."

"How long have you been hunted?" Togo frowned.

"Togo," I said, warning.

"I don't know. I..." Maude wrung her hands, scooting closer to the fire. "My Gift was revealed shortly before I was kidnapped and sold. After I was trafficked to the east, no one seemed to know there, and I killed the chief before he could harm me, and I ran, and then I've been with you since."

"The chief might have kept it hidden when you entered the land," Togo mused. "How was the gift revealed?"

Maude squirmed, struggling for a moment. I wanted to tell Togo to stop talking, but Maude needed to communicate — we all did, even if it hurt.

"We'll help," I said. "Don't be afraid."

Maude nodded. "I was raised in a small village outside of Norkid, in the mountains, and we all followed Creator. No one, however, was Gifted, in any form. But it was evident I had this Gift from a young age, and the village encouraged me to use it in private... I was... respected by some but..." She shivered. "I was hated by most..."

"Villages tend to hate their own, no matter how divinely led." Togo frowned. "How was it revealed?"

"The leaders did not like what Creator told me," Maude said softly, "and I... fled, into Norkid, alone."

"Alone?" I tensed. Norkid was not safe for a woman to travel alone, but judging by the forlorn heaviness in Maude's eyes, she knew that dearly now.

"I was taken there." Maude looked away, forcing another weak breath as she said, "But I did not wield the Gift after that — no one could have known to kidnap me in

Norkid if they did not first go to the village and discover my secret."

Righteous anger filled my chest. Someone in the village had sent men after Maude? What could they have hoped to gain by hunting her down? The people had taken Maude away — was that what the villagers had asked, or had they wanted Maude to be brought back to the village, and the hunters had not obliged?

"Then you cannot return home," Togo said. "Why did you go along with our intentions to return you to Norkid then? You could have gone anywhere else. Someplace far away, where no one knew your Gift."

Maude shrugged, tears falling down her pale, grimy face. "I miss my family. Is that a sin?"

Her words stung me. "Of course, it isn't," I said. "But we cannot take you to the village, or Norkid, if you'll be hunted, Maude."

"What else do I have? I was going to run and hide until my father settled the matter within the village — then I could return." Tears dripped down her cheeks and hit the blanket around her shoulders.

"You cannot." Togo sighed. "They will not be talked down by anyone if they have already sent people after you... It is not safe."

"I have nothing else!" Maude's voice rose in the still morning atmosphere. "I have no one else. I cannot start over anywhere — why would I? I cannot forsake my family —"

"Then you've been given another vision?" Togo asked.

Maude's jaw dropped slightly. "How—"

"You would have no other reason to rush home if you had not been given another vision. Your family is in danger, aren't they? That's why you're desperate to return and save them... No?" Togo tilted his head, piercing gaze unyielding.

Maude sobbed and dropped her head into her hands.

Her lack of answer spoke volumes.

I sat beside her, speaking gently. "Please let us help, Maude. If you need to return home because Creator gave you a prophecy as a warning, then there's time for us to help."

"It's not safe. You need to stick to the plan — let me go to Norkid alone. I'll go to the village and handle this." Maude spoke through tears.

What was holding her together, but the grace of Creator? She was a million broken pieces grasping at desperate hopes invoked by Creator — and to most, that would be a pitiful sight, but to me, it encompassed the goodness of Creator.

Because we were all this broken and lost, but only few had the love of the Light holding them together, truly.

"We can help," I repeated. "Please—""I already owe Togo a debt!" Maude cried. "I cannot afford more, Bjorn! And it's dangerous."

"Dangerous?" I blinked. "If you're talking of the hunters, well, we've already faced them down twice now, haven't we? I don't think any others would stand much of a chance against us."

"She does not mean more hunters or traffickers," Togo said simply.

His ability to know without telling me was grating my nerves. Couldn't the bastard communicate and let me in on whatever the hell was going on?

"What then?" I glanced at Maude. "Whatever it is, we can handle it, you know."

"Wizards," Maude said softly. "The wizards are seeking me, too."

TEN

"Wizards?" I frowned, sweat growing in my palms.

No.

Not again.

But was Creator not a God of irony? Of pushing a man to insanity and beckoning him to choose understanding, yet still?

"Yes," Maude forced. "I don't know their names for certain, or where they came from, but... But Creator warned me in my dreams, and then the man that bought me — he said he had a good token against them, and..." "The wizards will stop at nothing to gain you as a pawn. They are desperate for Gifted — and since your body is weak, they'll use that against you, to gain you as their ally."

"I won't help them!" Maude said through tears.

"They could heal you easily," Togo said.

"I don't care! I'd rather be sick than be healed by magic!" Maude spat.

I squeezed her arm. "It'll be all right. We'll figure this out. If the wizards are hunting you, then we'll just... find a safe place for you."

"There is no safe place," Togo said. "You'll need to find some sort of organization or alliance with a stronghold of Gifted in order to seek sanctuary and support. You could run to the ends of the earth, and the wizards would not give up the search if they thought it meant using your visions against their enemy, which is, of course, you."

"Then let them chase me." Maude wiped her eyes, anger rising. "Let them! I need to get home — I won't let traffickers or wizards stop me. I won't fail my family. They're all I have."

I understood the feeling, and the crisis. But if I had anything to say over it, this situation would go better for Maude than mine had gone for myself.

"We'll handle it," I said. "There is one organization in Buacach that accept Gifted — we can go there?"

"I need to go to Norkid! *Soon*! I can't waste time seeking sanctuary!" Maude insisted.

"What was the vision?" I asked softly. "Do you know for certain how much time you have left?"

Maude faltered before whispering, "I-I think so. I think I have another month."

A month of traveling on horseback still put us very close to reaching Norkid in time. We still had vast grasslands, rivers, and mountains to cross before we reached the north. And with hunters on our trail, we would possibly have to avoid main roads and cities, which would slow progress greatly, too.

"We would not be a good ally against the wizards if they are waiting at the village," Togo said. "You would need help..."

"How can I ask any organization to aid me when I am a total stranger?" Maude asked.

I cringed. She had a point. I knew the organization in Buacach was a solid, upstanding one — they trained countless Gifted in the ways of their Gifts and of Creator and would aid any soul that needed it — but it was still suspicious to request aid and travel for our situation.

"Then you choose to go in alone?" Togo frowned, head tilting again.

"I must. I cannot wait to gain alliances — and I cannot risk harming anyone else. I don't want you or Bjorn to follow me either," Maude said firmly, tears subsiding, replaced by a solemn determination.

"We'll join you," I said.

"The debt—"

Togo held up a hand. "Let's finish the mission and see what the debt looks like then."

"Mission?" Maude blinked a few times.

"You two will help me kill the prince of Norkid," Togo said, "and then we shall save your village. We'll have time to do both, if we travel correctly."

"Kill the prince?" Maude winced. "But he's..."

"It must be done," Togo said, "by me, or another, and it might as well be us."

"Why?" Maude sat frozen as if we had poured a bucket of water over her.

"The city is lost. Thousands more will die if he tries his childish games," Togo said, "and besides, a mercenary does not question orders. We simply do the job."

We. I gulped hard, not liking how he said that. I wasn't a mercenary. I was a man of Creator.

Then again... I was traveling with a mercenary... The Black Angel, no less. And I was going to be a partner in crime, wasn't I?

Creator, please, show me what to do — how can I protect Maude alone? But to keep Togo's support, I need to do the mission with him, do I not?

Creator did not speak to me. Did not give me a nudge in any direction. Why was He silent now?

Why had He led me to meet Togo, and Maude, if He would abandon me when I needed His guidance the most? I couldn't kill anyone. Not again.

But if I did not keep Togo's alliance, how could I save Maude?

"I can't kill anyone," Maude choked after a long silence.

"And you won't. Neither of you." Togo nodded. "However, if you both wish to leave, you may."

"But the debts..." Maude trailed off, looking away. "We cannot live in debt..."

But could we be accomplices to a murder? Was that any more Creator-like of us to do? Of course not. And yet, Maude and I both held some unspoken need to remain by Togo's side.

I prayed, and asked Creator to show me if I may leave Togo, but I couldn't, and Creator said nothing of it, so here we were.

No matter what — if I had to carry more bloodshed, I would, if it meant protecting Maude, and somehow, eventually, bringing Togo's damn soul to the light.

Creator help me. I couldn't give up now. I only prayed He would guide me before I made too big of a mess of things.

My gut, though, said things were already a mess, and it was doomed, as life was, to only go downhill from here.

ELEVEN

We traveled steadily for almost a week through the grasslands, keeping to the edge of the marshlands, but leaving distance between us and the Red River, too, in case we ran into traffic — or hunters.

As the week passed, we talked more and more. Maude told us stories over the campfires. Togo, too, wound tales of his times roaming the lands — though he kept his stories appropriate, I could tell. He didn't describe kills or anything too morbid. Maude would listen intently. I would sip my coffee and try not to dread the mission ahead too much.

After all, Creator blessed us with occasional moments of peace, such as this week, and I thanked Him for that.

But Creator remained silent. I still had no idea what to do.

So we traveled on.

The sun set slowly that evening, filling the sky with streaks of red, orange, and purple. We made camp beside a small creek. Maude washed up in the water while Togo and I set up the tent (we didn't use it during the storms to ensure it didn't tear or rip) and made a fire. Togo began dinner, and I went over to Maude at the creek's edge.

"How are you feeling?" I asked quietly.

Maude stood, watching the clear waters skirt over rocks and pebbles. Fish darted in the shallow depths. "Tired," she said honestly. "But I'm not in much pain today." She rubbed her shoulder. "Thank you for asking."

"We're making good time," I said, "but I also don't want you to push yourself too far and harm yourself."

"I'll be all right," she said. "Don't worry." Maude glanced past me and toward Togo. Lowering her voice, she said, "Bjorn..."

"Yes?"

"I don't want to kill anyone. I don't know what to do. If I run now, I won't last, and I know, and I won't be able to save my people alone. But to kill one for the sake of my village does not seem like something Creator would condone, either." She looked back toward the water, wiping at her eyes quickly.

"I do not have a solid response from Creator regarding our situation, either," I said. "But I think our guts are saying to continue on for now, so we'll take it a day at a time, yes? Please, don't worry too much. Creator will guide us."

How easy it was to say such things! It was far more difficult to believe them myself.

"Right." Maude nodded, flashing a smile like she always did. "I'm sorry. You're right." She started back to camp, glancing back as she laughed. "Clean up before you eat. You smell worse than roadkill."

"Thank you, m'lady." I bowed, smirking, and went to wash up. Once I finished scrubbing the dirt from my face, beard, arms, and hands, I went back to camp and sat beside Togo.

We ate a small meal after I said a prayer — Togo didn't close his eyes, but he didn't eat till we finished, either —

and chatted until night fell. Then we got our packs, and sprawled out under the stars beside the fire.

Maude fell asleep first. I looked over at Togo when she was asleep. "Togo?"

"Hm?" He sat beneath a tree, keeping guard.

"How many Gifted have you known?"

Togo sighed. "Why do you ask?"

"I'm just curious."

"I don't know."

"I have known very few." I mused up at the stars. "I think Maude has been the kindest."

"I suppose." Togo nodded. It meant a great deal to have him agree with me on the topic.

"We need a plan," I said.

"We have one."

"It's missing details."

"Most plans do."

"You're a professional mercenary. And the best plan we have is we'll kill a prince — somehow — and then save the village from... what we're saving the village from, we don't even know, but we know wizards will stand against us. And you're all right with the vague idea of a plan?" I sat up in the darkness, the fire flickering at my side.

"I am. We'll have a better idea of the enemy before we arrive. There's no need for wasted breath yet." Pulling his pipe from his pocket, Togo filled it and lit it.

"Why do you say that?"

"They'll come again."

"They will..." I sighed, rubbing my face, hating the idea of having to face more men and fight them, but we had no choice.

"We'll take one alive and question him," Togo continued.

I bristled. "Torture?"

"Aye." His tone held no hesitation. Or remorse.

"But..."

"We'll need to try." Togo shrugged and puffed smoke. "Maude and the village depend on us winning, do they not? The victors take the paths of the destructors, they only silence the enemy before the world sees the truth. We'll be like any other victor."

"I won't torture another."

"You are a hypocrite," Togo said.

I clenched my fists, glaring at him. "Because I try to live the life Creator asks me to?"

"You want to save the village and Maude, but refuse to lift a hand to harm anyone to do so. You cannot expect to win if you do not fight. Is Creator not a God of war?"

"He is," I said tightly, "but—"

"Then if you choose this battle, fight. If you do not, run now." Togo puffed more smoke into the darkness. "I will not beg you to do anything either way, but I will not carry you."

"I did not ask you to."

"Hm."

How could the man talk down to me after voicing that he already knew who I had been? Gritting my teeth, fighting rage, I said, "I am not afraid to fight or die for anyone."

"That is good."

"Are you?"

Togo eyed me. "I have no one to die for. Nor do I fear death."

"Then we are the same."

To my surprise, Togo did not argue, and watched the night silently, and I fell asleep until it was my turn to sit up and watch the campsite. He gave me a blade, and I took it without a word.

EARLY IN THE MORNING, something snapped in the forest. I sat up immediately, grabbing the knife on my side.

Togo sat up, silent as death, reaching for his own katanas, as another snap came out of the forest — footsteps moved low and heavy, growing closer.

Before I could move, the Black Angel lunged into the woods, and a split moment later, the *thunk* of a corpse falling came.

Scrambling to my feet, I jumped in front of Maude, knife drawn. Three men tore out of the forest, their swords drawn and piercing the air as they ran toward me. I parried one sword with my blade, dropping my weight down into my defensive stance. I didn't have Togo's agility — but I was big enough to put up a good fight, and that's what I would do.

The second sword swung toward my head, and I ducked slightly, stabbing my blade into the man's chest. At the same moment, Togo cut down the third man, and blood spewed over the grass.

Maude woke with a jerk as the corpse landed near her head. Shrieking, she immediately cupped her own hands over her mouth in vain, eyes wide.

"It's all right now," I said quickly, but I had no idea if was actually all right or not, but we would kill more if we needed to —

Even if I had promised myself I never would do such a thing again.

Here I was, with blood covering my hand, the grass, the —

Darkness clouded my vision and I struggled to breathe, lungs constricting as if some great metal claws clamped around them, and my heart beat so quickly I thought it might explode.

"Are you hurt?" Maude gasped, scrambling to her feet and coming to my side.

My side? Why was she worried about me?

"I'm —"

"It's my fault," Maude said, tears running down her face. "This is my fault — I'm sorry! I'm so sorry!"

Grimacing, I grabbed her by her arms. "Calm down."

"We should move," Togo said firmly, cleaning his katanas and sheathing them without another word, his lack of concern for the situation grating my nerves. Did he actually have a soul? Or had decades of hellish living waned his spirit to an ice cube or something?

"We should," I agreed. "Come, Maude." Releasing her arms, I sheathed my knife after wiping the blade off on my pants — a bit more blood staining my clothes didn't change much now — and saddled the horses with Togo. Maude packed up the camp, but she kept dropping things as her hands shook and she fought to control herself.

Seeing Maude in such a state ached me, but there was nothing to be said in this moment: and I didn't know what to say, anyway. It was, of course, a priest's job to encourage the struggling and wield whatever words that Creator gave them in the moment.

Well, Creator gave me no words of comfort. He gave me no instruction. He hadn't for some time now — had I done something to offend Him and keep Him away from me?

The Letters said that Creator would show Himself to those that sought Him — and here I was, throwing my foolish self into whatever situation He insisted me to jump into, and then He went silent, as I fell into the heat of the battles? What had I done? I didn't understand any of this — and I knew, yes, the irony that man cannot understand Creator, but I didn't want to fail Creator by not grasping His instructions, and was that predicament not a good, sensible one?

In silence, we mounted the mares and started off, leaving the corpses in the mud.

WE ATE SOME JERKY as we traveled, and finally, Maude spoke first again: "I'm sorry. I should have known they were coming —"

"The Gift does not work that way," Togo said.

"It should," Maude argued, and I'd never seen her rage before. Not like this.

Why was she so upset? We were unscathed, after all.

Togo didn't reply, but I said, "Please, Maude. We're safe — we handled it, yes? Please, don't —"

"I am causing you both to kill!" Maude's voice grew strained. "Do you not understand —" She stopped herself quickly, wiping her eyes.

"It is my job," Togo said.

But I understood Maude's words. Her pain.

She felt guilty and ashamed because we were protecting her, no matter the cost.

"Your life is worth this, Maude," I said softly.

Maude tensed. "No, it isn't."

"Then consider it this way: we are protecting your village, in a sense." Togo frowned.

"But your lives are not worth less than a village," Maude said angrily.

"I think you people put yourselves in conundrums to remain miserable," Togo said matter-of-factly. "We killed. We accept it. It does not bother us. So it should not bother you." Togo said nothing more, and I winced, but Maude's expression weakened.

Did she believe him? Did his harsh words offer some sort of respite?

"He's right," I said. Of course, killing did bother me, but I was also grateful to protect Maude's life, so I would do it again. Besides, I did not want Maude worried over it.

Maude fell silent, and we traveled the rest of the day without a word, which was very different from our long days of tales and banter, and the day wore on my heart more than I wanted to admit, as I avoided looking down at the blood stains on my clothes.

TWELVE

After another week of travel, things returned to normal — or as normal as they could be.

"Let me cook," Maude said. "You're burning it." Swatting me away from the little campfire, Maude took the wooden spoon from my hand and stirred the rice herself. Her brow furrowed in concentration as she salvaged the meal before it turned into something Sheol itself would barf up.

I sat down beside her, sighing. "Sorry."

"Did you never cook for yourself?" Maude asked.

Wincing, I said, "Of course I did."

"Not well, then."

"No, not well," I agreed. "But I survived, somehow."

"You're a large man to cook so poorly." Maude teased.

It was the first time I had heard her joke since the deaths that harsh night.

"I suppose," I said, "it is a bit ironic, but we'll blame it on my genetics, then. You're hard pressed to starve a draft horse." I joked.

"I suppose," she teased back.

We ate quietly after that, however, and Togo lit his pipe up after we finished. We washed up in the creek, and Maude and I said our prayers quietly, then we turned in for the night under the vast sea of stars, with the cool air biting us down to our bones. We would need more supplies before we continued on our journey.

Sure enough, in the morning, after a fitful night of sleep but a night without unexpected attackers, Togo made breakfast and announced, "I'm going into the closest village today before we continue on."

"We'll need blankets and more rations," I said. "And Maude needs a weapon."

Maude flinched, but nodded. "I can repay it, when... when it's all over," she said meekly.

Togo rolled his eyes and asked, "What weapon do you prefer?"

"I... I've never used anything but a bow and arrow, and I... I've never been good at aiming." Maude glanced away.

"There's reason you took to a poet's life, then," Togo mused.

Was that sarcasm?

"I can learn," Maude said.

"It'll be safer to find you a sword and train you with that," Togo replied. "You, too," he said, eyeing me. "Priest or not, a man must be armed. Didn't the Letters say so, even?"

"For a mercenary, you know many scriptures," I mused under my breath.

"Every killer knows the gods quite intimately."

"If you knew Creator intimately, then you would not kill for pleasure," I said softly.

"Who said anything about pleasure?" Togo puffed smoke.

Sighing, I changed the topic. "Do we have enough coin for the supplies we'll need? Or do I need to get work for the day? I have a blade, so I don't need more..."

"We have enough for now," Togo said.

"You're going alone?" I asked.

"Aye. You'll stay in hiding with Maude."

Maude sighed. "I'm sorry I can't help..."

"It wouldn't be safe," I said.

"I'll get you a cloak, too," Togo continued. "To hide your face so we can begin paying for inn rooms. This cold will grow worse, and there is no need to weaken the body further for no good cause."

I nodded a bit. "Right..."

"We'll keep a steady, harsh pace," Togo said with a sigh, "and giving our bodies the occasional break will keep us strong."

I didn't like the talk of preparing for the war that lay ahead, but Togo was correct, and I could only nod again.

Maude took a slow breath, plastering on a smile as she said, "Thank you. Both of you. I-I am certain that our efforts will not be in vain in the end."

The woman spoke empty words that clung to slivers of hope far out of her own reach.

Still, yet, I respected her for it.

I think it was braver to hold onto slivers of hope that could break apart in a heartbeat than to never hold onto anything at all.

After we cleaned up camp and fed the fire a bit more, Togo left with his pack and his cloak up over his head. Maude curled up beside the fire, under the blanket, reading the Letters. Her pale face scrunched as she focused on the lines of old text.

I kept watch on the forest for enemies, and ensured the fire didn't go out. The cold breeze shifted through the high grasses around us, and I made sure the campfire didn't get out of bounds and start a random fire. Maude fell asleep, face smooshed in the blankets. I carefully closed the book and tucked it into her pack so it didn't get wrinkled or dirtied.

I sat in the cool silence and prayed.

I prayed for Creator's guidance, for Togo's salvation, and for Maude's healing and comfort.

I didn't know if Creator would heed the latter prayers, but He did not respond right away to the former prayer, so I sighed softly and just watched the trees and grasses for a while.

After a couple hours, Togo returned. His pack hung heavier, and he carried a wrapped shortsword under one arm.

I stood hastily. "How did it go? Did anyone recognize you?"

Togo dropped his hood, a scowl of utter disgust on his face. "Did you just ask the Black Angel if a group of villagers recognized him?"

"Sorry, dumb question." I frowned.

"I got the supplies we needed," Togo said, squatting with the pack and opening it. "I even heard a rumor of Maude."

"What? People are speaking of her, even here?"

"It's funny, isn't it? Supposedly, she is a nobody, a weakling that the gods themselves rebuked, and yet, now she is vastly wanted for all of the wrong reasons."

"I would not say it's funny," I said sharply. "Far from it. Maude wants to be left alone, and she did not ask for this —"

"She did not ask for her Gift, which is courtesy of your God, yes? So why are you so quick to judge the wizards or mankind for wanting Maude for wrongdoing, when it is your God's fault she is not safe and sound to begin with?" Togo's piercing eyes met mine.

Anger lit in my chest — but what good would my anger do? Togo was not a follower of Creator, and I could not expect him to think or rationalize like one, so why argue with him?

I want him to understand, I thought. *But I cannot bash him into belief.*

I remembered many times where I had been able to show people of Creator's love. I had prayed with them and welcomed them into the Light's kingdom with open arms. Some had been difficult to help, some had run into the Light with no looking back.

But no one had ever been this difficult.

But Creator had told me to stay with Togo, had He not? I had not misheard. Had I?

After a long minute passed, I finally said, voice quiet, "I do not think Creator cursed Maude with this Gift. Nor do I believe that any person, whether they be considered, in humanity's eyes, a slave, a peasant, a lord, a king, is truly a nobody. I think we are all equal in the sight of Creator, and all have a vast, extraordinary life to live, if we may yet believe it and yield to it."

Togo shook his head, warming up beside the fire. "Clearly you believe such things." He gestured toward the pack. "Look over the supplies."

I did so silently. He had purchased all we needed and then some. I wondered how much money he had left, but decided not to think too much on the matter — he was the Black Angel, after all, and though I hated the idea of using money earned from bloodshed, I had no choice if I wanted to travel quickly to save Maude and her village.

Maude woke with a small start, sitting up quickly as she slowly calmed her breathing.

"Oh, good. You're awake. Here's your new cloak," I said, pulling it from the pack. "It's thick wool — quite warm." And expensive.

Maude took it with shaky hands. "Thank you," she said, glancing at Togo. "Very much."

"We should get going." Togo stood from the fireside. I closed the pack and put out the fire.

Togo tacked the horses and we mounted quietly, heading north once more.

THIRTEEN

On the first night out of the grasslands, a harsh cold settled over the forest we entered. The trees shook in the growing winds, and dark clouds billowed across the sky above.

It dawned on me, in horror, that we faced a snowstorm, and it was too early in the season for such weather. I prayed that the wizards had not summoned some strange spell to worsen the weather — but if they had sent hunters after us, would they not try to delay us in this way, as well?

Stomach knotting at the thought, I rode my horse closer to Togo. "Do you think this is the wizards?"

"I do," he said.

"We should seek shelter before it begins to storm," I said, glancing back at Maude. Her pale, freckled face lifted to the sky, cloak falling slightly as snowflakes fell around her.

We were already too late.

"There's a village at the foothills," Togo said. "We'll arrive in time, if we hurry."

We picked up the pace, and Togo led the way through the thickening trees. Maude shivered beneath her cloak, and our breaths turned to white clouds in the cold air as snow drifted around us. Snow stuck to the pine trees and ground, and I prayed that we would make it to the village before the storm settled in.

As it turned out, luck had seen the three of us begin our journey, and had promptly left for a lengthy vacation.

The snow fell harder, piling in heaps along the forest floor until inches covered the ground and weighed down the tree limbs overhead. Frigid cold bit at my face, and I pulled the hood of my cloak tighter but it didn't help. We forced our horses onward, their hooves crunching in the snow, our cloaks flickered in the wind as it picked up.

"A-are we going to make it?" Maude asked, voice small over the howling winds that rattled the branches above us, causing snow to plummet and dance.

Togo forced his horse along. "Keep moving."

The screeching wind made the horses skittish, but we kept them steady, guiding them through the worsening snowstorm. The white stuff blinded me — I couldn't see far ahead of us, though even if I had known these woods well, a snow storm would weaken and kill even the best woodsman.

The harsh winds, heavy snow, and the cold would kill us before we knew what happened if we didn't do something fast.

After a few minutes, Togo slowed. "Up ahead," he said over the winds.

I drew my horse beside Maude's. Maude slumped over a little, making herself as small as possible against the cold winds. I reached out and squeezed her shoulder firmly. "Almost there, Maude. Come along!"

Would she have a flare now? What if she passed out or wore herself out in this cold or —

"Aye!" Maude nudged her horse and we followed Togo out of the woods, and down a small foothill.

In the little valley, lights flickered in the darkness — cabins, buildings, and, Creator be praised, a few levels of lights that must have been the inn Togo mentioned. Smoke billowed from a few chimneys — I smelled it in the air, anyway, mingling with facefulls of snow and icy winds that chapped my skin.

We hurried through the snow-covered streets and stopped in front of the inn. Dismounting, I helped Maude off her horse, trying to shield her small stature from the elements in vain.

"There's a barn out back. I'll rub down and feed the horses." Togo stepped over and took the three horses by their reins, then shoved coins into my freezing palms. "If I'm not back in twenty minutes, come find me."

The barn could have been a mere ten or twenty feet from the inn building, and a man would still get lost and freeze to death in a blizzard.

"I will," I said firmly. Togo had never asked such a thing of me.

He had never entrusted his life to me before.

Without another word, I led Maude inside while Togo went to untack the horses in the barn.

The lobby of the little inn reeked of mildew and mead, but a large fire burned in the giant hearth in the center of the room, and an elderly woman sat at the desk to the right. Paintings, animal skins, and lanterns hung on the wall behind her.

"Welcome to Sage Inn," the woman smiled, "though not to be confused with the Sage Clan," she waved us inside hastily. "Shut the door, now, quick!"

I slammed the door shut behind us. Maude shook hard, hugging herself tightly. In the light of the fire and lanterns, her pale face turned ashen. "S-sorry," Maude said.

"You're quite all right, dearie. Come, you're both going to freeze to death — let's get you warmed up, real slow like, now." The woman, short and round, with long white hair braided in two thick braids down her back, hurried over and ushered us to the hearth side.

I sat Maude down in the wooden chair that the woman pulled up. Maude shivered, her teeth chattering hard. That was a good sign, at least.

"Let's get these cloaks off," the old woman said, sliding Maude's off promptly, "yours too, sir. I'll hang them up."

She took mine and hung both cloaks over another chair. Then she removed our shoes and told us to sit closer to the fire. "Don't get too close. Warm up slowly. There, that's best."

I sat beside Maude in another chair, holding my hands out to the big, bright fire. The heat hurt, but I rubbed my hands and arms, then glanced at Maude. She did the same. I wondered if this cold hurt her more than it hurt me. Neither of us had frostbite, that I could tell by looking at our hands or feet, which was a blessing, but while I would bounce back easily from the cold, would she?

The old woman talked nonstop, and I tuned back in to listen. "I'll go put on some soup for you both —"

"Our friend is still outside, er, untacking the horses in the barn, I hope that's all right," I said. "If he's not inside soon, I'll have to go find him." I reached for my boots.

The woman waved a hand at me. "It is no problem — but Creator help him! This blizzard came so quickly, and it's unlike any I've seen this early in the season! I wouldn't want to be out in it even for a moment. How far did you three travel in it?" She pulled a few blankets from a large wooden cabinet near the desk and brought them over. Draping one over Maude, the woman continued, "Not too far, I'd hope, but judging by how cold you both are, you definitely came further than the outskirts of the village, hm?"

"Y-yes ma'am," I said, "we've traveled for miles in the snow... We were in it when it began."

"It is a miracle you are not losing fingers." The woman waggled a finger at me after putting the second blanket on me. "Now, sit here. I'll be back, and for Creator's sake, if your friend doesn't return, yell, because I can send my grandson out to fetch him!" She hurried off into the back room behind the desk.

I shifted in my chair, pulling the blanket that the woman had put around me a bit tighter. "Maude? Are you all right?"

"Yes," Maude mumbled, "just cold."

I shivered, glancing at the big, wooden door. "I don't know if I want to wait the full twenty minutes..."

The fire crackled and popped. Maude lifted her head, her red hands shaking as she wrung them on her lap. "Maybe not..." Concern laced her words.

Before I could yank my boots on and return to the elements, the front door opened, a gust of wind and snow piling in around the tall, thin form in the entry.

"Togo!" Maude gasped in relief.

I stood quickly, bare feet aching from the cold still, and went over. "Come sit down." I grabbed Togo's cloak off of him before he could argue.

Togo sat in my chair, and I pulled another chair up beside him. He sat heavily, sweat pouring down his face, some of it already freezing to his temples. I knelt quickly and removed his shoes.

Togo scowled a little, shoving me away. "I've had worse." He kicked his feet out so they were within the warmth of the hearth, rubbing his hands in front of the flames, too. The fire cast light over his face — and for once, he actually looked a little unsettled.

"Are the horses all right?" I asked.

"Yes." Togo didn't look up from the fire.

"You don't have frostbite, either," Maude said, peering over Togo's shoulder. "That's good. I'd say we're all very blessed, considering."

Togo's left eye twitched. "Considering," he said tightly.

Maude turned back to the fire, murmuring, "Are you sure you're all right?"

So then, she saw the same unsettled look in Togo's eyes that I did?

"We're losing time," Togo said solemnly. "This blizzard will put us back greatly. We might lose the mission, and the village."

I sighed, shaking my head. "The blizzard has to end — we'll continue, even in the snow, yes? It'll just slow us down some, but we'll make it."

Togo shook his head, but before we could continue the conversation, the old woman returned with a large wooden tray hoisted over her shoulder. Three bowls of steaming soup, and three mugs of steaming liquid, sat on the tray, along with chunks of black bread.

"Here we are, sip these, yes? You'll feel better in no time — it's my secret recipe, you know. My grandmother made it for me during blizzards, too!" Smiling a dimpled-smile, the old woman set the tray on the table beside me, and she handed out the bowls of soup first, dunking a chunk of bread in each bowl. "But do take it slowly!"

Togo practically growled at the old woman's kindness. "How much extra will the meal cost? We paid for a room —"

I cast him a look, though he didn't look over. "We can pay —"

"There is no charge! Creator's sake!" The old woman fetched another blanket and promptly draped it around Togo's shoulders. It was like watching a woman put a doll's dress on a disgruntled kitten. "Creator has much to say about helping those in need! What sort of old witch would I be if I charged you for a meal during such a snow storm? Humph, child!"

Maude sipped her soup, slumping slightly in the chair as if the warm liquid eased something deep inside her. Good soup had a very extraordinary effect on people. "What's your name?" she asked softly. "I'm sorry, we've been so rude—"

"Not at all, dearie. You've almost died out there, and when one is in survival mode, pleasantries fall to the wayside, and rightfully so. You can call me Nana."

"Nana," Maude repeated. "I'm... Maude."

"And I am Priest Bjorn," I said gently, offering a hand, holding the hot bowl of soup with my other. "And the grumpy one is Togo."

"It is wonderful to meet you each," Nana said with a smile. "Now, eat, and warm up, and I'll prepare your room. Then it's off to bed for you three — we can't afford anyone falling sick." With that, the old woman vanished into the hall beyond the lobby, her footsteps light on the wooden floor.

I glanced at Togo. "You should not bite the hand that feeds you."

"The hand that feeds you is usually the one that chokes you," Togo hissed.

"She's at least one hundred years old!" I snapped. "She can't choke anyone!"

"It's not a literal saying —"

"Shh!" Maude hushed us. "Don't bicker."

Togo and I fell silent and dropped our heads like insolent school boys. "Sorry," I said. "Anyway, we should discuss the plan — is there anything we can do to avoid delays, Togo?"

"I cannot control the weather. I am not a wizard."

I rubbed my face and eyed the fire as it lapped at the big, slow-burning logs. "The wizards know we're in this area..."

Togo scooted closer to the fire, chair squeaking on the wooden floors. "They might not know we're in this village specifically. We might have time to move out after the blizzard, but we also might be trapped here, and they could ambush us anytime."

Maude forced more soup down, tears glinting as they ran down her face, but she did not make a sound.

I winced. I did not know the people at risk in the village, but she did, and every moment that we were here, the heavier Maude's burden became.

FOURTEEN

Nana led us to our room, chattering like a songbird as we walked. "There are two beds, both warmed and ready, so you just go on to bed now, and if the storm grows too dangerous, I'll come wake you, and we'll all move to the cellar." She held the lantern a bit higher with a calloused hand. "Yes?"

"Yes, ma'am," we said in unison.

Nana smiled and nodded. "Good."

I opened the door, and Maude and I thanked her again, while Togo offered a very small bow, and then we crowded into the room.

A big fire burned in the hearth, and the beds were piled with clean blankets. A basin of fresh water sat on the table, and a few changes of clothes — two pairs of men's clothes, and a dress for Maude — lay on the beds, too.

Togo hung up a clothesline in front of the hearth, and we kept our eyes averted, so Maude had time to strip the wet clothes off, and dress in the new, warm gown. Then she sat beside the fire and gave us privacy while we changed clothes, too. We hung our clothes to dry on the line, the water slowly pittering to the wooden floors.

Our bellies still full from the hot dinner, we sat around the fire and kept our voices low.

"We need to leave now," Togo said.

I cringed. "Leave? But we sought sanctuary because we'll die out in the storm —"

"And if the wizards find us here?" Togo asked.

They would harm Nana, no doubt.

But what other choice did we have? I shook my head. "If we left now, they would probably still come here, and demand our whereabouts from Nana. Even if we did not tell her where we went, they would harm her for the information, anyway. It is best to remain, and fight to protect these people, if we have endangered them."

Maude hugged her knees, the fire illuminating her eyes. She was terribly silent.

Almost like...

"Maude?"

"They won't come tonight," Maude said softly. "We should sleep while we can."

Togo and I exchanged a brief glance. "You've been told this?" I asked. "Your Gift says as such?"

"Aye," Maude whispered, and said nothing more, which I didn't find very comforting, but I couldn't push her to say more.

Togo stood. "Very well then."

I tensed. He trusted her Gift that totally? "Er, I can sit up and watch —"

"Sleep," Togo said, "since she says it is safe." He laid down on the bed closest to the door without another word, pulling the covers up over himself and rolling over with his back toward us.

Maude stood on shaky legs and sat on the bed closest to the window. She gave me a reassuring nod, before burying herself in the blankets.

Head aching, I sat on the bed opposite of where Togo lay, and rubbed my face. The wizards could come during the night and slit our throats — but between the three of us, maybe one would wake before it happened? Then again, we had not seen Maude's Gift fail us yet — still, it could happen. It was my job to ensure she was safe, and if I failed her...

I curled up under the blankets, passing out before I could give the matter any more thought, as the exhaustion of the day — and the relief of a warm bed — settled in.

AFTER A WHILE, I woke from the same nightmare and sat up in bed. The wind howled outside, and I slipped out of bed. Peeking out the thick curtains, I winced at the heavy downfall of snow.

The world was white, but it looked to still be nighttime, though it might just be the dark storm. It felt like it was night — I had not slept for long. I never did.

I went over to the basin, splashing some water over my face. Using the towel on the table, I dried my eyes and looked back toward the window. The storm could last as long as the wizard needed it, most likely, so we wouldn't outrun it, or wait it out... We were truly stuck here until the wizards found us.

And what other option did we have? Leave and freeze to death in the elements? We wouldn't make it far, even if we weren't stopped by wizards.

Yet, still, if we stayed here, we could not fight armies of wizards — we didn't know how many were actually after us. But it was safe to assume there would be many wizards after us. We would be outnumbered. And outskilled.

The Black Angel had killed many, outwitted many, outskilled many — but he had never mentioned going against wizards and magic. He was a powerful mercenary — but he was not a magic wielder, or Gifted, and between us, no matter what we did, we were hardly a fair fight against a few wizards, and certainly less against many.

Still then, after all of the odds stood against us, why had Togo gone to sleep?

I glanced over at him, still sleeping under the covers. Did he trust Maude that much? Did he not believe a Gift could be faulty?

The wind picked up and the windowpane practically shook. Flinching, I stepped over to draw the curtains, as if that would slow the damage if the glass shattered.

Maude stirred in her sleep, mumbling softly. I looked back at Togo. He was sitting up in bed, eyes piercing mine. Eerily silent.

"Togo, perhaps we should move to the cellar?" I whispered. "The weather is worsening."

Togo shook his head.

"It isn't safe —"

"It will be all right."

I rubbed the back of my neck and paced the floors, careful to avoid the squeaky boards so that Maude did not wake. "Why do you sleep?" I asked before I could stop myself.

"Because I am tired," Togo said dryly. "It is exhausting work, defending two fools night and day."

I clenched my jaw. "No. I meant — do you truly believe in Maude's Gift? You think it is so flawless to put your life in it? You cannot possibly trust us that much. It makes no sense."

Togo looked toward the door, lips in a thin line. "It has not guided us wrongly yet."

"We have not tested it greatly. Do not lie to me." I pressed him. "Why were you so quick to rest in such a dire situation? It's unlike you."

"What would you rather I do? Sit up and worry about the future?"

"We usually take watch!"

"We are at the end of this road," Togo said firmly, "and the next step will be battle, so we needed some rest. It is a part of war, Priest. To sleep among crimson snow before the dawn brings another battle is part of being human." He tilted his head. "You know this more than anyone."

Blood boiling, I turned and faced him, gesturing at him before I could control my rage. "Do not speak of my past again!" I seethed through my teeth, trying to keep my voice low.

"It is your own fault we are in this mess — you are what happens when a man attempts to flee the truth," Togo said. His words revealed the truth I had tried to ignore for so long.

"I will not return to who I was," I snapped. "I am a new creation made in Creator — no one will make me resort to what I was!"

"Not even Maude?" Togo asked.

Whirling on my heels, I faced the hearth, the warmth of the flames hitting my sweating face.

I did not answer him.

"You lie, even to yourself," Togo said.

"I will do what it takes to help her, and her people, but I will not become my past self. That's where you and I diverge, Togo. You consider yourself a monster, and do monstrous things, but you do such to become a monster — you flee your own spirit. Is that any better than me fleeing my past self?"

Togo shook his head and stood. "I know Maude's power is great — she has not been wrong before. She has said such. But we are stuck here, and it is time to admit our defeat."

My stomach dropped. Skin going clammy, I said, "What? But you're the Black Angel, you've never met defeat!"

"We need to outwit them." Togo stretched his arms over his head. "But it won't be easy."

"What if we use me as bait?" I suggested.

FIFTEEN

"Bait? Pardon me?" Togo tilted his head.

Dismay gripped me. Surely, Togo had to have a better plan than tossing me out into a blizzard in some wild attempt to lure the wizards after me? But apparently not, because he asked what I had in mind.

So I plunged in. "If I leave the cabin, and they think Maude is with me, it gives us time to fight them away from Maude..."

"But Maude cannot go with you." Togo stepped toward the fire, leaning one hand against the wall and looking down into the flames.

"The innkeeper has a son —" I pressed on. "What choice do we have but to try and lure the wizards away?"

"It would not work," Togo said with a sigh.

"Why not? I don't hear you coming up with a solution." I crossed my arms over my chest. I towered over Togo and was much broader than he was — but it still felt like I was a mouse facing a lion.

"If they even fell for the trap, you would be killed, and the innkeeper's son promptly taken. There would be no fight — they are magicians, and they control this storm. Your vision would be impaired and you have but a sword." Togo huffed. "Shall I continue as to why that plan is foolish?"

"Then you come up with something. We can't just sit idly by and wait to be hunted." I clenched my jaw, rage building. No, not only rage — determination. These wizards had us in a corner. And I would not be a victim again.

Especially not now, with Maude and her people counting on us.

Togo sighed. "We'll face the wizards head on when they give up the storm and find us here, or when they find us traveling, depending on the blizzard's state, and we continue from there."

"You just said it would be futile to fight wizards," I snapped. "How is that plan any better?"

"Because it's mine," Togo replied smoothly.

"Togo!"

"You are one man with a blade. I am another with my blades. Maude is not skilled, and is more of a hindrance with a blade, but is still able-bodied. Now, if they attack here, the innkeeper, her family, and the people dwelling in this inn will be endangered, so they will either fight, or hide, and that shall be up to them. All of this against a group of wizards is not a good probability of success — but we have something else that will help us win."

"What?" I asked. Togo spoke in roundabout riddles — and I had no patience for it. Deciphering Creator's parables in the Letters took enough mental stamina as it was. To sit through Togo's babblings was downright infuriating. Though, that was probably what he thought of my rambles, too, so perhaps we were even.

"Do not worry about that. Let us prepare. I have a feeling they will come soon." Togo sighed, stepping away from the hearth, shadows falling over his face. "A pity."

By the way he said that, he did not sound as if the attack would be pitiful for us. It almost sounded as if he felt sorry for the wizards that would ambush us.

But he had already said our numbers and chances were weak — so why did he feel sympathy for the enemy? Or was it not sympathy, but something else? Something sinister?

Did Togo know the truth about me? Was he hinting for me to step forward and admit the truth? Especially in such a dire situation as this?

I took a slow breath. "Togo, as you know, I have not been entirely honest with you..."

But before I could explain myself, a loud *bang* echoed from beyond our bedroom door.

SIXTEEN

Weapons drawn, Togo and I hurried toward the door, and Maude jumped upright in bed.

"I'll stay with Maude —" I began, but Maude grabbed her shortsword from its sheath and stumbled after us.

"I'm going!" she hissed. In her new, loose dress, with her long hair tangled in a bun and bags under her angry eyes, she might scare the wizards away just by the sight of her.

Togo didn't argue, though I half-expected him to, and slipped into the hall. Another bang echoed. It came from the lobby. Had the wizards blown their way through the front doors? A cold draft raced down the hall as we crept toward the lobby.

A few doors opened behind us, and people poked their heads out, wide-eyed. "What's going on —"

"Stay in your rooms," I said. "Hide!"

The people slammed the doors shut in response.

The inn was full of people — innocent people.

How many would die tonight just because we had entered the abode?

As we approached the lobby, lanterns lit up the room, and footsteps sounded on the wooden floors. There was a whole group of them by the sound of it. How were we supposed to fight so many men without casualties? *Creator, help us, please,* I prayed. *Save the others.*

A booming voice pierced the inn: "Where is the Gifted woman? Give us Maude, and we will go peacefully."

My gut clenched. Could I take Maude and run, despite the blizzard? Well, even if we made it far outside, the wizards would just kill the innocent people inside.

But surrendering Maude was not an option.

So if we could not run, or surrender, that left a fight.

Creator, forgive me.

But what else do I do?

Another voice came. "You'll do no such thing!" Nana scolded sharply. "Now, get out! You are not welcome here!"

My heart lodged in my throat as Togo and I stopped at the edge of the hall, just out of sight of the crew of wizards standing in the lobby room. I spotted Nana near the men, but she held no weapon — dammit, why didn't she have a weapon to defend herself with? What was she thinking?

A tall man, with long, sleek black hair hanging past his waist in a thick braid, smiled down at Nana. He wore the all-black uniform of an Order wizard — and held a long, golden staff in his left hand. "You are the owner of this inn?" he asked softly. "And you would willingly die for a stranger such as the woman?"

"You wizards have no right taking another soul as if it is worth nothing." Nana didn't step back as the wizard reached out. He cupped her wrinkled chin. Nana's small hands clenched, and she said, "If you wish to shed blood on my property, you will have to shed mine first."

I ran out of the hall. "Wait!"

The group of wizards turned their heads to glare at me. The tall man flashed a smile, but did not release Nana's face. "Ah. The priest. Bjorn, isn't it? Or should I call you by your other name at a time such as this?"

"Maude isn't here," I blurted.

The wizard sighed. "Do not waste our time. Send her out, now. Or I'll kill every single person in this building."

His threat was not empty — but I couldn't surrender Maude.

"Let's make a deal," I said hastily. "Please —"

"I have no need for a deal." The man lifted his staff slightly, and a bright, yellow light glowed from the head of the rod.

In an instant, the light struck Nana's chest, and she crumpled at the man's feet, never making a sound. Blood poured from her eyes, nose, and mouth, pooling on the inn's wooden floor.

A scream erupted behind me. A ragged, broken cry, almost like a child's.

The tall man stepped over Nana's body, smiling brightly, his eyes glaring at someone behind me. "Ah. Come along, Maude."

I stepped back, stretching my arms out to block the hallway where Maude stood gaping and sobbing now. "No! Take me instead! Leave Maude." Stomach twisting,

I scrambled for the right words to say. "My Gift is far more powerful than hers —"

"This might be so, Mabuz, but she is weaker than you." The man extended his right hand toward Maude.

As soon as the wizard spoke my name, hot, white rage engulfed me.

I became no one.

I tackled the wizard to the ground with inhuman strength, and lights flooded the room. The wizards wielded their magic of all kinds, of all skill levels, but none of it touched me.

Screams erupted in the inn. I didn't know who they belonged to. But one was so loud, so close, it must have been mine. I wrapped my hands around the wizard's throat, and he struck his golden staff against my head, but it didn't faze me.

I squeezed tighter. Tighter.

Yells and cries and bangs and thuds echoed all around. The cozy little inn had turned into a battlefield.

The wizard's pale face twisted into a smile, and before I could finish him off, he disappeared from underneath me.

Teleportation.

He was a high level wizard — of course he could teleport.

I scrambled up, yelling like a raging lion. "Maude!" Bodies littered the lobby floor — wizards with gaping, bleeding wounds caused by blades.

Maude stood over a body, her shortsword dripping blood. She shook like a leaf in the wind, but she lifted her head, eyes meeting mine. Tears ran down her face.

"I'm sorry," she said, her ragged voice barely above a whisper.

Then she collapsed.

I stepped forward and caught her swiftly, holding her close among the wreckage. The lanterns on the walls sent light dancing and flickering over the wizards' bodies — and a few bodies of the men resting at the inn that had rushed to help us, disregarding their own lives to protect their loved ones.

The wails of those said loved ones filled the air. Women and children rushed to gather their fallen, sobbing and beating fists to their chests, kneeling in the blood of the dead.

Still blinded by my rage, I turned to Togo, carrying Maude in my arms.

This was my fault — it was all my fault.

Togo was right.

Togo didn't speak. He went down the hall, returned with our bags, and then I followed him outside before the reality of the situation settled in and the people turned on us, too.

SEVENTEEN

It had ended almost as quickly as it began.

In the moment, as we fled the inn and trudged on the backs of our horses through the thick drafts of snow, I had no time to think of it. I only held Maude tightly, while her horse ponied mine, and tried to keep her warm by tucking her under my cloak, too.

But as the sun came out, and glimmered and danced over the snow that settled over the land and barren trees, realization sparked in my soul.

Togo was not Gifted, as I was, and as Maude was.

Still... He showed no fear, though he also did not seem heartless: he had displayed pity on our enemy before we slayed them.

It was why he was the legendary man of myth, the Black Angel: he did not need a Gift to be the legendary killer.

I hadn't seen him in action like that before. But I understood the name now.

The sun glinted across the forest of pure snow. The eerie silence that dwelled only within snowy worlds hung heavy, but I broke it. "Why didn't you tell me that you were Gifted?"

"Why didn't you tell me that you were Gifted?" Togo asked, voice quiet.

"I told you. I left it all behind." But there was no anger or indignation in my chest. Only a strange sense of defeat.

"You have not."

"I cannot. Not now. You were right, in a sense." I looked up at the sky. The morning sun combated the white and gray clouds.

"I usually am."

"But when this battle is finished, I think I will be, too," I said softly.

I said nothing more. I did not need to.

There are many things better left unsaid between warriors. There are many things that are left unspoken and yet understood.

We left the hills behind and entered the mountain range by nightfall.

Togo and I didn't speak for a long time. When Maude woke, she reacted similar to how she had before: apologizing weakly, as if the entire ordeal had been her fault. I reassured her gently, as we dismounted briefly so she could eat a bit and drink some water, that it had not been her fault, and that Nana had known what she had been putting herself into.

But Nana had done it anyway — to protect us.

I could not let her death be in vain.

"We're growing closer to the village," I said softly. "Nana will be proud of us by this journey's end. Keep heart, Maude." I squeezed her shoulder and stood.

Maude stood from the log, brushing snow off her cloak with shaky hands. She was still in her gown, but we had covered her up with a few layers of clothes before we had started the trek the night before.

Without a word, Maude nodded. She mounted her mare, and we followed suit. We pushed the horses onward, down the narrow dirt path, which was mostly mud now.

But the snow and frigid cold had all vanished after the morning. The wizards hadn't kept the veil of weather up since they were all dead, of course.

Well, most of the wizards that had attacked us last night were dead.

That one, the leader, had vanished. Would he find us out here? Kill us? Take Maude? Or had he run off for reinforcements? We were past nightfall now, and had not had any more attacks, so perhaps the wizards were off our tail for now. I prayed so.

We stopped and made camp beside a small cave and a creek. In solemn silence, we boiled water over the large fire Togo made, and finally cleaned the rest of the blood from our hands. Maude changed her clothes in the dark cave, and came back out with her cloak pulled tight, shivering slightly.

Togo cooked dinner over a large fire he made, and I fished in the stream for extra fish to cook and store for our travels.

Maude sat silently. We ate together, but there were no stories or banter. I read the Letters silently and prayed, and Maude did, too, but tears ran down her face as she finished her prayer, and she laid down to hide under her blanket.

I laid down, too, while Togo took first watch. A lone owl hooted in the forest beyond, and the stars filled the dark sky above. The cool wind whistled through the barren tree limbs. The world was soft and quiet — as if it, too, wept silently like I did.

After a while, I fell asleep, and restless dreams took me. I was awake before Togo had to nudge me, and then took my spot as a sentry near the crackling fire.

I watched the empty woods. The horses grazed on some dead brush a short distance from the campsite. Togo slept soundly, and Maude stirred in her sleep, but I didn't try to wake her.

I wondered if she was having a nightmare.

I wondered if Togo was even capable of such a human thing.

But that was foolish of me — Togo was human, no matter how cold or calloused he appeared. He probably had worse nightmares than even I. If I wanted to reach him and help save his soul, judging him would do me no good.

But he irked me. Unsettled me.

He knew me.

He knew too much about me, when I had never even said a word of the truth, and of course, it was his job, just as understanding him was my job, too, but when you put two mercenaries, two broken souls, two lost, damned souls, together, you do not get a peaceful outcome.

But I think we had both known that the moment I started following him around.

Yet, neither of us had put any end to it.

Because, of course, what did two damned souls have to lose?

Togo lived as a shackled man feigning as a free man, and I lived as a free man feigning as a shackled man. Did it make sense? Did it represent the justice and love Creator offered?

No, because I was damnable, and even when I tried my hardest, I could not save every life, nor could I wash the blood from my hands — and yes, Creator had washed me crimson, but my mind was another matter, was it not? — and I could not live a life that truly encompassed hope. Did men see me and think, "Ah, yes, he has found something to be cherished! I want this Light that he has!" Yes, some men had. But others had seen my laughter, and my kindness, and my love, and had said, "Aha! He is a fake! He is as broken, and as sad, as I am! I do not need his lies to live this life."

And I am afraid, deeply, morosely afraid, that both men were right — and that I was, perhaps, truly nothing but a sham.

I had led lives to the Light. But I had not led many others. I had joy in my heart. But I was still a broken man.

To be a follower, a lover of Creator, did that mean that a soul must be white as snow and never know pain?

Were all of those men correct, and I had been misled in my expectations of perfection? Because no amount of my trying had fixed me as a person. And no amount of faith in Creator had truly made me a new person, had it?

I was still me.

Broken and distorted and ashamed and blasted.

Was I a new creature? Truly?

Or would I fall back to my old ways?

Togo's voice tore me from my reveries. "I think it is time to prepare our plan. We're getting closer to the kingdom now."

"You have a plan for the... the killing of the prince?" I asked quietly. The reminder of our fate made my stomach churn and guilt and repulsion clawed at my heart. I did not want to kill any innocent man. I would not. Not again. There would be some other way to save Maude and her village, even if we had to walk away from Togo now — even if we had to die with our debts never repaid.

But was there? Was there any chance at successfully saving Maude's village without Togo's help? And we could not gain his aid without accompanying him on his blasted mission.

"Yes," Togo said.

Maude shifted uneasily in her saddle, glancing over at Togo with a pale face. "W-what is it?"

Tilting his head, looking up at the tree branches shaking in the wind, Togo said, "I think we should kidnap the prince instead."

EIGHTEEN

With only a week remaining, we arrived at Norkid with low rations, tattered, muddy clothing, bruised and scarred skins, and weary but hopeful spirits.

Or, at least, my spirit was weary yet hopeful, and Maude seemed the same. Her eyes remained heavy — but her optimism showed in her words, in her actions.

We were not giving up yet, though we all knew the risks ahead.

It had been months of travel and it all led to this moment, this mission, even if we had not known such at the beginning.

The mountains, great, vast, snow-covered mountains, opened up into a great clearing, and perched on the edge of the cold sea sat Norkid. It was a grand kingdom in size and stature. But the evil that lurked within it...

I shivered, pulling my cloak over my head a bit tighter. "Almost there now," I said. "Right on schedule, too." I tried to sound reassuring.

Maude nodded once, eyes staring at the city below the mountain we trudged down. "Aye... Almost."

In silence, we continued our trek down the mountain at a snail's pace. We dismounted for most of the journey, letting the horses find their own footing, taking it slow so they didn't harm themselves. We crunched through frozen mud and piles of snow. The eerie silence on the mountainside was not lost on me — but I filled the nerve-grating silence with mental prayer, hoping to remove some of the anxiety.

It didn't really help.

But alas.

At the bottom of the mountain, we let the horses take a small break. We ate the last of our rations and drank the last bit in our canteens, and then mounted the steeds again. We reached Norkid as the sun began to set beyond the kingdom's horizon. Bright reds and purples slashed across the paling sky.

The guards at the gate didn't bother asking us who we were — I was unsure if they knew, or if they did not care. I doubted they knew us — what with our cloaks up high, and my beard and hair hiding my identity some, and Maude covering most of her face with her shawl to ward off the cold. We didn't look suspicious, though but we also didn't look as inconspicuous as others, but what else were we to do?

Togo led us onward in silence. The horses' hooves clacked against the cobblestone streets as we moved north, toward the heart of the city. The city was winding down: smithies closed their doors, mercantile men hurried home, and most of the homes we passed had smoke coming from their chimneys as people hid from the crime dancing about them, like herds of mice averting their eyes from packs of rats.

The only places open at this hour were the inns and saloons. We passed a few of each — they were all as I recalled them. Packed, loud, and a few even larger than before.

You're not a street rat anymore, I told myself. *You do not fear these men.*

And then, *these men fear* you.

But that reality did not comfort me as much as I used to think it might.

We traveled through the city with our heads down, but we remained vigilant. Even now, so shortly after the sunset, evil ran rampant.

A woman's cries echoed from one alley, followed by a man's gruff threat.

Togo cast me a look, then one toward Maude, as if to say, "You cannot save another. Not yet."

We rode on. My stomach twisted. The thump of the hooves beneath us clamored in my ears. My heartbeat quickened as snow drifted around us, little white flakes that stuck to the stones of the street and buildings' window panes.

In the shadows of the alleys around us, wickedness ensued. It was as if mankind thought a few pieces of brick and mortar could keep Creator Almighty from seeing their sins. And what was I doing? I ignored it all tonight — to save Maude, and the village, but was that not also a sin? To deny the protection of a few tonight, for the protection of many in the village?

Hands shaking, I craned my neck as something small and black flashed in the street to my left.

A boy scurried out of the shadows. He held something small in his left hand, and he ran toward me and my horse.

I immediately reined Flower, my mare, to the right, running her into Maude's mare slightly, pushing them back from the boy's attack. "Wait," I said quickly. "I'll give you money."

The boy slashed at my mount but didn't come too close: he wasn't trying to harm us, yet, only trying to scare us. As if a boy weighing perhaps fifty pounds soaking wet could intimidate two grown men and a woman.

"Give it to me!" the boy demanded. "Hurry! Everything you have!" The desperation in his voice tore a hole through my heart.

I had been him.

No. I am him, even still.

"No." Togo pulled his horse forward calmly, one hand on a katana, but he did not withdraw it. "I can cut you down before you're able to move another muscle, child. Now, run away."

The boy's face paled even further, but he gripped the little blade in his hands tighter. Lifting the weapon upward toward me, he said again, "Give me your money, or else!"

Or else? He could stab the horse, maybe. But I could just as easily kick him away or tackle him or cut him down. Did the boy not see he had no chance against us?

He knows his odds. But he has no other choice here.

"Togo, wait," I said hastily. "Boy, here." I pulled a few coins that Togo had given me out of my cloak pocket.

Bring him. The voice itched my gut.

Creator spoke to me now? Of all times?

Well... All right, then.

The boy stumbled forward, reaching out one hand for the money while the other hand held the weapon like a lifeline. But before he could snatch the money away, I leaned over from my mount and snatched the blade from his hand. Even using all of his strength, he couldn't withstand me.

Gasping, the boy reeled back, but I jumped off the horse swiftly, holding him. "Wait," I hissed. "Let us help!"

"Priest, let him go," Togo scolded. "We need to move. Have you forgotten the mission?"

"He can help!" I insisted under my breath. "He's small — we could use his help, and we can pay him!"

Maude gasped. "Bjorn! It isn't safe!"

The boy wriggled in my arms, but then he froze. "How much?"

"What?" I asked.

"How much money does it pay?" The boy didn't even know what *it* was. And yet, interest coated his words.

"A lot," I said. "It wouldn't be very dangerous. But you have to come with us tonight. Can you do that?"

The boy hesitated briefly, then shoved at me. "Let go."

"You're crazy," Togo snapped. "Let's go. Now. Leave him with the coins." He turned his horse's head away.

"I'm in!" The boy squared his thin shoulders, glaring up at me. "I'll do anything, just let me get the money! Promise! Or else!"

"Deal!" I nodded firmly. "Come along."

"What about your master?" Togo asked. "He won't take kindly to you running —"

"I have no master!" the boy snapped indignantly. I reached down and put him on my horse, then mounted behind him.

"Bjorn..." Maude whispered, fear heavy in her voice, but she didn't rebuke me again.

Huffing, Togo led us forward again, picking up the pace a little. The boy clutched the saddle horn and I kept as far away from him as possible on the back of the horse, careful not to touch him much while I held the reins. He sat rigid.

Our breaths making white clouds in the air, snow falling like all was perfect and silent, we hurried through the vile kingdom until Togo stopped us at a small tavern called The Broken Keg. A few men vomited off the front deck, and a few others smoked against the railing, but it was surprisingly quiet inside the tavern — maybe we could actually get some sleep instead of being woken by noise and singing all night.

We dismounted our horses out front of the tavern and inn. I took the packs quickly and shouldered them. Togo eyed me, eye twitching as he shoved coins into my hand.

"Get a room," he ordered, "and a meal." With that, he led the horses around back to the shelter.

Maude kept close to the boy, and I led them inside, giving warning glances to the men we passed outside.

In the tavern, men gambled, drank, and smoked. One man lay across a table asleep, but no one moved him. A few of the waitresses gave me hungry side-eyes, but they tended to their regulars, and I resisted the urge to put a hand on Maude and the boy's eyes.

Maude put a hand on the boy's shoulder, whispering to me. "Is this the safest inn in town?"

"I assume so, if Togo led us here," I whispered back. "Stay close."

I went to the front desk and promptly paid for one room and a meal for four. The man eyed the boy and Maude, then me. "Even the priests need a good time every now and then, eh?"

Rage ignited, and before I could control myself, I lunged across the counter and snatched the man by his starched shirt collar. "I am no such vile creature as that —"

Maude grabbed my arm. "Bjorn!"

The man laughed nervously. Had I been any smaller, or weaker, I'm sure he would have kicked me out of the inn, but for whatever reason, he didn't. "It's only a joke." He pushed my arm away, and I stepped back.

"I... apologize," I said through gritted teeth. "It's been a long journey. My sense of humor is weary."

The man chuckled and handed me the key to our room, adding, "Your meal will be brought up. My treat." His eyes twinkled in a way I despised.

But I could not afford to make a scene.

Dammit — all I did was dig myself graves, didn't I?

"Thank you." I led Maude and the boy through the inn and into the hallway. We found our room quickly, and we filed inside. Locking the heavy wooden door behind us, I sank against it a little.

Maude patted my arm. "It's all right. No harm done. We should be fine." She pulled her cloak off and put it around the boy's shoulders. "Here. You sit down and rest a bit. We'll get the fire started."

The boy's face contorted at the sudden motherly affection. Shaking myself, I moved toward the hearth and took some kindling from the box nearby. In moments, I started the fire and fed it some larger logs, but my hands shook. Had they been shaking since the boy found us?

Pull yourself together. You're in Norkid. But you're not helpless anymore. This time is different. You have people counting on you to protect them, so you can't afford any weaknesses.

I glanced over, clearing my throat. "My name is Bjorn. This is Maude. What's your name?"

The boy stood stiffly in the center of the room, between the two beds, the cloak hitting the floor. Maude was short, but the boy was even smaller, and he had to be at least ten years old.

"Iggy," he said.

"Iggy, it's nice to meet you." I stood and offered a big, calloused hand.

The boy eyed it, distrust in his sharp brown eyes, but then he shook it as firmly as he could. "When do I get the money?"

I sighed. "Well, we're... doing a mission."

How much could I tell him? He was still a street rat and couldn't be entrusted with our entire tale or mission. But he was going to work for us, so he needed to know enough to complete his tasks.

"You're mercenaries?" The boy's eyes widened and darted between Maude and I. "Real ones? How many have you killed? Kidnapped? Are you really a priest? What are you?" He gaped at Maude.

"Shhh!" I shook my head. "Keep your voice down!"

"You *are* real mercenaries!" Iggy whispered.

Maude shot me a look, sitting on the edge of a creaky bed tiredly. "Maybe we should wait till Togo comes back..."

"Is he the Black Angel?" Iggy asked, pulling the cloak around himself closer. "He looks like him. I've only heard rumors, but —"

"Quiet down," I repeated. The boy wasn't talking that loudly at all, but the idea that we might be understood by a mere child sent shivers up my spine.

Iggy clamped his mouth shut.

"We're not mercenaries, nor is Togo the Black Angel," I said. "Our mission is nothing so dramatic."

"Well, what is it?" Iggy's shoulders fell.

I paced the dim little room. "I can't say."

"Because it's important?" Iggy asked. "I won't tell anyone a thing!"

"Shh!" I insisted.

Someone knocked on the door and I tensed, hurrying over. "Who is it?"

"Let me in." Togo's tight voice sounded.

I opened the door quickly and locked the door behind Togo as he entered. Togo hung his cloak on a hook on the wall, sighing. He reeked of disapproval. But I knew I had done the right thing: I had to help the boy, and we needed his help, too.

The mission wouldn't be easy. And a small street rat would aid immensely, whether Togo admitted it or not.

Iggy inched closer to Togo. "Are you the Black Angel?"

Togo glanced down with narrow eyes. "What do you think?"

"You are." Iggy wriggled in his soleless shoes. "Then who are they? No one ever said you had help!"

"I don't." Togo sat in a chair beside the hearth. He said nothing, but Maude looked into a pack and handed him his pipe. Togo's eyebrows knitted but he mumbled a thank you.

"Then why do you need my help?" Iggy asked eagerly.

Togo scowled. "We don't." He eyed me. "The priest is a soft-hearted fool."

I glared, but the boy spoke up, "I don't need charity. You give me a job. I'll do it. I can earn the money!"

"You were going to steal money," Togo rebuked. "I do not believe the word of a thief."

"Well, you're a mercenary, that is worse than a thief!" the child argued, clenching his bruised fists.

"It is." Togo lit his pipe.

I stepped forward. This was getting out of hand. "Listen," I said. "We're going into a place where a small mole like you," I gestured to Iggy, "will be much help."

"In the entry?" Maude whispered, realization hitting her face.

"Yes." I nodded. "And he'll be safe and sound, too. It won't endanger him greatly."

Togo puffed smoke. Iggy grinned a half-toothless grin. "I can do it! Anything! Where are we going?"

"Well, we'll be breaking into the castle," I said.

NINETEEN

Once our tentative plan was told, Iggy ate the meal that was brought to us — Maude gave him her biscuit, though we didn't let him eat too much to make himself sick — and washed his face in the basin, then promptly fell asleep in one of the beds.

The adults present exchanged looks.

The fire cast shadows over the little, stuffy room.

"Well," Maude broke the silence, "I think he'll be all right, and perhaps he can come with us, and he can stay in the village — safely, away from all of this... vile city."

"You both live in a fairy tale," Togo chastened. "You've dragged this boy into a dangerous mess he doesn't belong in."

"You agreed to let him help us," I said tightly. "And we won't let anything happen to him. But he's too small and weak to last long in these streets, and you know it." In a sense, as terrible and twisted as it seemed, we were saving him.

What a harsh reality this was: casting a soul into one precarious situation saved them from some other cruel fate. It didn't seem right. But it was part of the world we lived in. And I couldn't sit idly by and let others succumb to evil if I could do something, anything, no matter how desperate or small, to try and give them a new, better fate.

Togo sent a cloud of pipe smoke into the air before saying, "It makes no difference to me."

I rubbed my face and sat on the other bed. "We'd best get some sleep. We have a long day tomorrow."

Togo and I took the bed closest to the door, and Maude curled up in the other bed, giving Iggy plenty of space.

I prayed silently, passing out before I could finish.

PALE MORNING LIGHT CAME through the window pane. Maude and Iggy slept soundly in their bed. Maude looked so peaceful — even Iggy seemed to look like a child instead of a furious urchin.

Togo had already gone, and I assumed he'd gone to get breakfast or was already on a supply run. I had heard him wake before the sun, but I hadn't followed.

I finished dressing and splashed water on my face from the basin. When I turned around, Maude sat up in bed.

"Good morning," she mumbled.

"How are you feeling?" I asked.

"The same as usual," she said, but judging by her pale face and shaky hands, she felt worse than usual.

I gulped, but nodded. "I'll go fetch some breakfast."

Maude pursed her lips. "Bjorn?"

"Hm?"

"Are you all right?"

The question almost struck me as funny. "I am as well as any of us are," I said. "Remember — take heart. I know it seems like reality is more confusing in the light of the dawn, but it will settle out, and all will be fine." I forced a reassuring smile as if to lift a fist of defiance in the light of the morning that flooded through the curtains.

Maude straightened, nodding slightly as she said, "Aye. Of course, it will be fine. Thank you, Bjorn. I cannot ever truly repay you for your help — or Togo for his — and I'm accepting that now, but... I shall try and do whatever I can, anyway." Resolve shined in her eyes.

I shook my head. "You needn't worry about that, Maude."

I donned my cloak and slipped out of the room, locking it behind me. I went to the lobby quietly, avoiding the morning crowd as men and women hurried to get their meals or leave the inn with their luggage in tow. Smoke filled the air, and even in the bright, early morning, a few men sipped mead or whiskey.

I ordered a few breakfast meals from the woman taking orders in the front of the lobby, and then I waited quietly at the counter. I watched as men finished their night-long games and gambles before they filed outside, too drunk to walk properly.

Rubbing my beard, I took a slow breath. So far, no one recognized me. Of course, they wouldn't, but it was still a deep-rooted, irrational fear of mine. No one would have any reason to assume that small street urchin years and years ago was now a big, burly monster.

Besides, this inn had not been one I frequented as a child, so I was still relatively safe.

The bartender from the night before gave me a weary glance, but smiled nervously when I met his gaze, and he hustled back to work. I had lost my temper and it could have ended much worse then — I couldn't slip up again.

I pictured Maude, with her laughter, and joyful stories, and shining eyes.

No more weakness.

I pictured Togo, and his unspoken words, and his undecided fate.

No more mistakes.

I pictured Iggy, and Maude's village — innocent victims of evil's cold grip.

No matter what, I won't fail them.

The waitress returned with a platter of food, and I gave her a coin as a tip, then hurried off with the platter. I knocked on the bedroom door, and Maude let me in.

Iggy, washed up thoroughly now but still wearing his tattered clothes, peered up at me. "Smells good," he said.

I put the platter on the table. "Help yourself."

Maude put a heaping plate of sausage, eggs, biscuits, fruit, and a glass of milk before Iggy, then sat beside him. Maude prayed a brief prayer before picking at her own plate.

I ate my food silently, letting uneasy silence fall over the three of us, and the silence was broken when the door opened and Togo stepped in. He locked the door behind him, eyeing me. "Good morning."

"Good morning," Maude and I said in unison.

"We'd best get going." Togo dusted some snow from his cloak and put his hands in front of the fire.

Iggy shifted in his seat, zeal lighting up his face. "We're going out already? But I thought the mission wasn't until tonight?"

I sighed, ruffling Iggy's hair. "Don't question things too much."

Togo pulled some clothes from the pack he carried and tossed them at Iggy. "Put these on."

Iggy stared at the clothing. "I can't pay you for them…"

Togo scowled. "What is it with the lot of you being so determined to fulfill debts? I thought that was only my culture." He waved the boy off and closed the bags crossly. "Let's go now."

We waited, giving the boy as much privacy as we could by stepping into the hall while he dressed. A few minutes later, he stepped out, wearing black pants, a plain gray tunic, and new shoes. He wrinkled his nose. "The shoes pinch."

"*You're welcome*," Togo corrected, heading down the hall.

Maude smoothed Iggy's unruly black hair. "Come." We hurried after Togo.

Snow piled in the streets. I recalled that at one time, some men had cleared the streets during winters, but if such men still worked for the kingdom now, they must have been slacking today.

Wagons and men on horseback created ruts in the snow, melting parts of it. Smoke filled the air from the countless puffing chimneys. The barren kingdom appeared placid, but after the horrendous previous night, I knew just how cruel it truly was. It was even crueler than I remembered it to be.

We left our horses at the inn and went to the castle on foot. Well, Togo went to the castle. Maude, Iggy, and I stayed in the surprisingly busy marketplace. I couldn't help but wonder if our plan would work. Usually, mercenaries used their setting to aid their quest — a festival, a coronation, such events like that were perfect opportunities to kidnap a prince.

But we had no luck on our side. And, Creator forbid, I doubted even Creator was on our side — but surely, He understood the situation, and knew that we were doing the best we could to avoid any unnecessary deaths. Or did the ends not justify the means? It was difficult to tell, but at this point, I was in too deep to give in now, and kidnapping the prince was surely better than killing him, which was what Togo was paid to do.

Shaking my head to clear my thoughts (as if it would help), I turned to Maude and Iggy. Maude looked over the supplies the traders laid out in their booths. Even in the snow, the marketplace was alive. Women and children, wearing shawls, coats, and gloves, sifted through the aisles and purchased necessities. Men carried goods to and fro from wagons and buildings.

Iggy walked with his head down, but there was a slight vigor to his step I hadn't seen before. His eyes shined ever so slightly, too. It was confidence, wasn't it? The type of confidence a soul bore when they believed to have a place in the world.

Hiding a smile, I glanced down at Maude. "It's almost time for our midday meal, don't you think? Why don't we treat Iggy a little?" I nodded toward a small pastry shop down the road.

Maude grinned. "Aye."

After all, why not? Iggy would live on, no matter what, but we might not be here after another week. Why not have a pastry?

We made our way through the streets, which due to the snow, weren't terribly busy, and crowded into the little pastry shop. It was dimly lit, with big windows at the front, and a small sitting area with chairs and tables. Candles flickered on each table, and the sweet scents of chocolate, cinnamon, and sugar flooded my nostrils.

A large man waved at us. "Evening! What can we help you with?"

Iggy inched over to the display cabinet. Goods of all colors, shapes, and types lay in rows behind the clear glass covers. Practically drooling, Iggy gaped at the sweet goods.

Maude spoke politely with the pastry chef, and I watched Iggy with a smile. After a long moment, the boy pointed toward what he wanted, and Maude ordered two of them for him. She also ordered two small coffees and pastries for us, too. She paid him promptly, seeming more relaxed than I had seen her in quite some time.

Beaming, the man nodded. "Please, take a seat."

We sat in a corner booth, and I kept my back to the wall, watching the door. Togo still had a couple of hours before he would return, and then we would prepare for the mission.

The baker brought our meal over on a tray. Maude placed Iggy's treat in front of him. Iggy had chosen a mug of juice, and he sipped it briefly before digging into his delectable food. Maude and I nibbled our sweets and nursed our coffee.

Men and women entered the shop, bought their goods, and hurried out, but two women entered the shop and sat with their treats. They were only one booth over. Try as I might, I could not help but overhear their conversation.

"You really think that he'll be killed?" the first woman, a slight, frail lady in expensive clothing, whispered.

"I don't think the king will surrender his position. What else can he do?" the second woman said with a shake of her head.

My blood boiled. So, it was true. The rumors of the prince's assassination were all over the kingdom. But did no one find it too sickening to repeat? Or, worse, did no one truly care enough not to throw a revolution? Was the kingdom going to sit idly by and let the innocent man be slain?

Maude rested a hand on my forearm, giving me a small frown. So she heard it, too.

"Poor prince," the first woman said. "I wish he could have restored this kingdom to what it was, but I suppose that's been ages ago. Civilization cannot stay stagnant."

"But the king is causing this civilization to burn into ruins," the second woman said with disgust. "We really ought to leave, hm? Perhaps Buacach would be a more welcoming kingdom — I hear they're very safe."

"I don't know if I can leave..." the other woman murmured. And the ruthless cycle continued.

No one truly cared that a life would be lost. They only cared that their kingdom was filthy. Yet, did they truly even care of that? If they cared, would they not take action? Would they not try to save their home, and the innocent lives that bled in the city's streets?

No. Of course, the kingdom was disgusting, and not just because of the thugs and government men in power — but partially also because of the people that did nothing —

they did no evil, but they did no good, and I think doing no good was equivalent to doing evil, even.

Maude squeezed my arm. "Iggy," she said, clearing her throat. "When this is over," she kept her voice down, "do you wish to follow us to the village where you can dwell?"

"Aye," Iggy said, his mouth smeared with white sugar. "I can do just fine there. Anything beats this place."

I nodded absently. Maude continued. "It will be safe when we... um, finish." We hadn't given the boy the complete rundown on what exactly we had to do with the village, but he had not asked. "You'll be happy. I was."

"Why did you leave?"

"I think grown ups just have to leave sometimes," Maude said, "but they usually return home, eventually, whether to a place, or to their family."

"Do you have a family?" Iggy asked, finishing his first pastry.

"I do. Parents, and a few sisters, and a brother," Maude replied. "They're all very nice."

"Like you." Iggy smirked. "I'd like to meet them."

Maude smiled, blushing. "You shall."

I couldn't help but relax at seeing her smile so genuinely. And anyway, I had never asked about Maude's family so directly. She had woven tales of her siblings' shenanigans on the ship for the crewmates to laugh at — but she had not given much more than that, and those had been stories. Her response to Iggy had not hidden behind any storytelling. It was the simple truth: Maude had family, and I was reminded, so harshly, that their wellbeing lay on Maude's shaking shoulders.

It did not seem fair. But I would help her and win, no matter what — the entire kingdom, the whole bloody world, could choose to rot, but I would die if that was what it took to ensure that Maude, and Togo, and Iggy, now, flourished.

Though, I hoped and prayed, I would live on, perhaps, and learn more of Maude's life, and Togo's as well.

I took a slow breath and let myself relax again. Sipping my coffee, I listened as Iggy and Maude chatted about her village. A soft gray haze covered the world beyond the big windows: snow fell softly, and the baker added more logs to the hearth in the room to keep us all warm.

This kingdom was vile. But it still held some good.

And that good had to be cherished, but most importantly, protected.

TWENTY

We approached the castle through the back alleys. Maude and Iggy kept close on my heels, and I prayed Togo would be waiting where we had planned. Of course, he was the Black Angel, so nothing terrible had happened. Most likely. He had probably gotten all of the information we needed to infiltrate that night without getting caught — he was a skilled mercenary, after all.

So why did my gut twist? The terrible feeling in my stomach refused to leave.

My gut was rarely wrong.

"Stay close," I whispered for the millionth time.

"Aye," Maude said patiently. "We're almost to the spot, yes?"

"We are." I sidestepped to avoid a gruesome puddle of something.

Maude sighed, glancing about. So far, no thieves had jumped us. *So far* being the keen part. "I pray he's made it back."

"Of course he has," Iggy said with a scoff. "He's the Black Angel —"

I cut him off. "Shh!" We didn't need the entire kingdom hearing about us.

Iggy sighed but fell quiet, inching closer to Maude as we entered another dark alley. Rats squealed nearby. I adjusted my cloak to keep my sword hidden, praying I wouldn't have to use it tonight.

And if I did, then Creator, forgive me.

After another minute of walking, we stopped in a small alley. Besides stacked crates and some litter, the alley was empty. It was only a short distance from the castle's entrance and stables: a perfect rendezvous spot.

Of course, when Togo returned, we would prepare the horses for after the mission. We would leave the kingdom with haste, and, if all went well, would have the prince in tow toward Maude's village long before sunrise.

But my gut nagged, and I prayed that things did go smoothly, for once, despite my concerns. The plan was, of course, not without its flaws, because while Togo was a legend, he was still human, and we were limited in manpower, abilities, and time.

After a long minute, a figure appeared at the end of the alley. Togo spoke immediately. "Ready?"

"Yes," I said quickly. "Is everything all right?" I couldn't blurt out my questions while we were in public, but judging by Togo's calm demeanor, I assumed nothing too chaotic had happened.

We were still on track.

"Of course." Togo led us through the narrow alleys without another word. Maude and Iggy kept on Togo's heels, and I took the rear, staying alert in case any enemy appeared from the shadows.

When we reached the stable behind the inn, the place was growing busy — men hurried inside to get their drinks and gamble their money, and the stench of alcohol wafted from the swinging doors. The snow continued falling, piling into the streets heavily. Perhaps the men thought they could drink away the cold.

I bristled as a drunk man stumbled off the inn's deck. "Hey," he said, waving a finger toward us.

We kept moving, almost around the side of the inn now. The man half-ran, half-stumbled over. "Hey, wait!"

"Can I help you, sir?" I asked while I pushed Maude forward slightly, and Togo continued walking.

The man reached for Maude but I stepped between them. "Can I help you?" I repeated sharply.

The man slurred, tilting his head, "I needs talk to the lady —"

"She does not wish to speak with you." I didn't let him pass me, though he tried again.

"I need to talk with her! Get outta my way!" He shoved at me, but I didn't budge.

I snarled, grabbing his arm and pushing it back painfully. "I said no."

Maude hurried around the side of the inn with Iggy. Good — at least Togo could watch out for them while they readied the horses. I just had to keep the man away for a few minutes. *Maybe I should knock him out,* I thought. *But it might cause a scene, and we don't need to cause scenes tonight.*

"Maude!" the man shouted through the falling snow.

My breath caught, and I shoved the man backward. He fell on his ass into a pile of snow. Shock twisted his face.

"Stay away from her," I hissed, "or I'll kill you."

The threat left my lips before I could stop it.

The snow fell in heavy torrents. Time froze. I stared down at the man and he stared up at me, his hands placed firmly on the cobblestones. We were locked there — waiting for the other to make the first move, to seal the other's fate.

Maude appeared at my side and she gripped my arm, her voice small, timid, as if she were afraid to lift it over the growing storm: "Ivar? Is it you?"

The drunken man raised both hands in surrender then, slurring over his passionate words. "It's you. Maude! It's really you! Where have you been? What happened to you? Please, come inside, I'll get you a drink, and we can —"

Maude spoke hastily, helping the man upright. "I cannot, cousin. Please, listen very closely. I must go with my friends, and you cannot tell a soul that I was here." She searched the man's rugged face with concern. "Promise me!"

The man, Ivar, presumably her cousin, scoffed. "Maude, don't be silly. You must come home with me. Let's get another drink and talk —"

I stepped forward. "Maude has made herself clear," I said. "Leave, now."

Ivar growled, his thick eyebrows furrowing as he rested a hand on Maude's shoulder. "Maude, who is this?"

"My friend," Maude said. "Please, Ivar. Listen to me. We have to go, but I'll meet you at the village very soon. Please. Go straight there and wait for me outside the hills!"

Ivar opened his mouth to argue, but Maude withdrew, and grabbing my arm, she tugged me behind the inn. Togo stood near the stables, with all three mares tacked and ready to go. Iggy perched on the back of Maude's mare, his cloak pulled up tightly to ward against the snow.

Maude mounted behind Iggy, and I mounted my horse, but I cast a glance back. Ivar stood and stared. He probably thought he was in some sort of stupor — but so long as he did not follow us, I didn't care what he did.

Togo sighed, mounted, and then urged his horse forward. Without another word among us, we began our trek toward the castle, leaving Ivar in the snow outside of the tavern.

This would be a grave mistake.

TWENTY-ONE

Outside of the castle, we hid our horses in a small, quiet alley. I could only pray they remained consistent in their training, and did not decide that tonight would be the night they decided to flee and leave us forever.

And then, we split up. Well, mostly.

Maude and Iggy would wait for us with our mounts in the alleys — if we got injured, they would man the horses for our escape. Maude had wanted to accompany us inside, but Iggy had, too, and we decided it was not fair to risk his life, so Maude accepted the new role for Iggy's sake.

Meanwhile, Togo and I would break into the castle and find the prince in his chambers. The prince's chambers were over the castle gardens. It put us quite close to the escape route to the alley, luckily. Maybe Creator was going to bless this outrageous mission.

The castle was surprisingly quiet. And forlorn. Ivy grew up the gray stones and parts of the once-grand towers lay crumbling now. While the castle was not the sign of power it once was, it was a breeding ground for wickedness.

The guards on the wall hardly paid any attention to their duties. After all, why should they? The kingdom was hardly a target, and so, most of the guards gambled and drank on the watchwall.

Meanwhile, Togo and I hid in the brush before we approached the gate. Togo unlocked the wooden gate swiftly: it was one entry rarely used, and the soldiers took it as a shortcut to the stables beyond the castle ground's walls.

One guard leaned over the edge of the great wall, but Togo and I closed the gate, pressing our backs against the wall. In the shadows, we were invisible. When the guard turned back to his pacing overhead, Togo and I ran silently toward the castle itself. Our footsteps made no noise over the stone pavement.

The gardens were unkempt, but in the winter, with snow covering the ground and dead trees, it hardly mattered if debris piled up here.

We entered the castle through one of the back entrances, which led directly into a large, dimly lit foyer. Togo closed the door swiftly behind us, and we crept to the left and down the hall. So far, so good. Togo had mapped out the guards' rounds, so as long as we kept good time, we would avoid the soldiers altogether.

We moved through the grand halls in silence. The castle of Norkid was old, and had once been well cared for and cherished — but now, dust caked the floors, the walls, the lanterns that stood unlit on the walls, and a dank, musty smell lingered in every corridor.

I tried to hold back a sneeze. Togo slowed around another corner, and then, he peered out behind the stone wall.

Then, Togo lunged.

I stepped out after him, and in a second, we dropped the two guards at the prince's door before they could make a sound or lift their swords. We slowly lowered their bodies so they didn't make any noise.

I moved forward, pulling a metal lock piece from my cloak pocket. While Togo watched out for any surprise guards, I picked the lock to the prince's chambers.

Click.

I nodded once toward Togo. I slipped the lock into my pocket, drew my blade, and opened the door. It made no sound, the wood gliding on well-oiled hinges, and I peeked into the room. It was large and luxurious, and a big fire burned in the hearth. The bed, with heavy comforters and more pillows than I had ever seen on one bed before, stood to the right. The prince slept soundly, sprawled on top of the covers without any clothes on, and his snoring rang in the room.

Well, he was there, at least, and not springing to attack us. He was caught unaware, and while that was a bad thing for a prince to have happened, it made our job easier.

Togo covered me as I stepped into the room. Creeping toward the prince, I took a slow breath. We had one shot at this. Everything hinged on it — if I slipped up, Togo might decide against mercy, and kill the prince, as he had originally been taxed with doing.

And I couldn't let an innocent life be taken.

I stood only feet from the prince's bed now. He was eighteen, and just as large a man as his father the king was, with thick blond hair and scars all over his back. I tensed. Where had he gotten all of those scars? The prince had never seen battle.

I pushed the thoughts aside and moved forward. Now, or never.

I clamped a hand over the prince's mouth and held my knife against his neck with my other. Instantly, the prince woke with a jerk, the whites of his eyes gleaming from the light of the fire across the room. His body tensed, he tried to strike me, but I pushed my blade against his skin firmly.

"Easy," I whispered. "We're here to save you from your father. There's a bounty out for your head, and we're offering you freedom."

The prince seethed, but I didn't withdraw my hand from his mouth.

"If you accompany us, you shall live. If you fight us, you shall die. Do you understand?"

Would he believe me? Did he know of his father's wicked bounty? Or would he fight me, regardless, and try to die a hero? The prince wanted to save his people — would he be willing to give that up in order to survive?

As cowardly as it might seem, I prayed he did.

The prince sat up a bit more, then nodded slightly under my grip. His eyes were forlorn — as if he accepted whatever his fate might truly be. He doubtlessly expected that I was lying, and that we would kill him, or perhaps take him off for hostage or torture.

"Dress," I said, withdrawing my blade. "We'll take you away from here safely."

The prince got up and pulled his pants and tunic on. He kept his voice low. "My father put the bounty out?" he whispered.

"Aye." I nodded.

The prince's hands trembled as he tugged his boots on and reached for his sword and scabbard. Togo said, voice low but sharp, "Let the priest carry the weapon."

The prince hesitated, but then handed the scabbard to me quickly. "Please don't lose this. It was the only thing my mentor bequeathed me." Desperation rose in his eyes.

"Aye, of course. It is yours as soon as we escape this castle." I strapped the extra sword to my body. "We must hurry and be silent."

The prince slid his heavy woolen cloak on with a firm nod, and then, we slipped out of the room.

We were almost there. Now, we just had to escape through the same way we came, and meet Maude and Iggy in the gardens.

We were still on time — we shouldn't run into any guards.

Togo led the way back into the corridor, his footsteps silent. The prince, unlike us, made a bit of noise as he walked, and I nudged his shoulder warningly.

Pushing through the dusty, dark corridors, we moved single-file, until Togo stopped abruptly ahead. The prince almost crashed into him, but I grabbed his arm to stop him.

Voices came from up ahead. Soldiers. They were not chatting or gossiping — instead, I heard a sharp, distinct, "We'd best hurry." The urgency in the man's tone was worrisome, and my gut twisted.

They know, I thought.

How could the guards know that we were here? Absolutely no one saw us when we entered!

Togo's shoulders relaxed with resolve. He would strike them down in seconds.

I couldn't let that happen.

But they were right ahead — coming this way, and we couldn't turn back and hide in the halls, nor could we afford to waste time with a detour through the castle.

The prince's breath caught, and then he pushed forward, past Togo. "Guards," he called out calmly. "What is this talk? Why are you worried so?"

The soldiers stopped in their tracks and I heard them shift on their feet. "Prince Balder," one soldier spoke quickly, "we have heard a rumor that the Black Angel and the Mabuz the Manic are within the castle walls... They may be out to kill you, my prince."

"And you four are the only soldiers that have come to protect me?" the prince's voice fell soft yet hard.

Realization hit me then: out of the thousands of men the Norkid army had, only these men had bothered to protect their prince.

Blood going cold, I kept silent in the shadows with Togo, praying the prince would choose to escape with us, and praying that these soldiers could be spared.

"I... I am sorry, Prince Balder," another guard said weakly. "You... you know how it is here... But please, come with us so that we may protect you."

"If the Black Angel and Manic are here, then four human men stand no chance against them," Prince Balder said calmly. "As prince, I am commanding you each to step down from this fight."

"But the coronation — if you can live till then, my prince —" the first guard fumbled for words.

"Then I shall only die in some other horrific way, and the throne will be returned to my father," the prince whispered. "It is time I accept this fate. But know this," and then he named each guard, "that I shall return for my throne no matter the cost, and when I do, you four had best be alive to see it."

Silence filled the corridor. At last, the sound of armor moving echoed. I looked around the edge of the corridor ever so slightly. Moonlight peered into one of the high windows, illuminating the guards. The four soldiers knelt before Prince Balder, their heads bowed low.

"As you wish, Prince Balder." The men spoke in unison.

Prince Balder knelt, also, and said again, "None of this will be in vain. Now, please, my friends, go."

I pulled back into the shadows again, my heart in my throat. The guards shuffled and after a moment, the hall was empty again.

Prince Balder stepped back over to us. In the dark, with only rays of moonlight entering the hall, I could not see much, and the prince kept his face turned to the shadows, but I figured he must be hiding tears. "Let us continue," he said firmly.

Togo took the lead again, but this time, our steps were faster. I didn't understand how the guards had heard the rumor tonight. Who could have told them about us?

Had someone found Maude and Iggy? Had they harmed them for information? Had they taken them, also?

Panic and rage clawed at my gut. I pushed even faster, until we reached the exit that we came from.

If someone had touched Maude or Iggy, I would rip them apart. I would —

Togo pushed the door open slowly, looking out. He gestured to confirm that we were clear. Then it was true — only four men had rushed to defend the prince, and the rest of the guards had kept to their routine we had already staked out.

We hurried through the garden grounds. The snow piled terribly high now, but we pushed through it, and I prayed that the others would still be waiting for us. If not, we would be too late, wouldn't we?

Togo whispered to us, "The cousin will be waiting for us. Be ready."

The cousin? My gut twisted. Maude's cousin, Ivar. Had he told the guards about us? And they had believed him?

It went farther than that, though. When we first met Maude, she had told us that someone in her own village had to have shared her secret — that she was Gifted. Had Ivar been the one to expose her from the beginning?

Rage burned hot in my chest, but I held it down for now. We raced through the gardens and pushed through the exit without any guards noticing us. On the wall above, as we passed beneath, men's laughter echoed. They called out and placed bets on how they would find the prince's body mutilated in the morning — they knew the prince was being hunted, and instead of protecting him, they betted on his death like men gambled on dogs.

I fought the urge to look at the prince. He heard his soldiers, doubtlessly, but he made no sound.

TWENTY-TWO

When we left the castle wall behind, my rage grew focused. We were almost to the alleyway now, and we raced over cobblestones and snow. I heard no ruckus — no screams, cries, or anything to let me think that a group of hoodlums had found Maude and Iggy. But was that a good sign? Had Ivar already found them and taken action against them?

Togo stopped at the entry of the old alleyway. He drew his katanas in the blink of an eye, and I pulled my sword as well, though I did not see why until I reached his side.

Ivar stood over Iggy's body in the alley, and in his arms, he held Maude by the tip of a curved blade. Blood fell from Maude's temple, and she shook hard, but jutted her chin defiantly.

"Let her go, now, Ivar!" I hissed.

"You two are going to leave," Ivar snarled, "and I am taking Maude to the village where the wizards can have her as they see fit!"

He was going to sell his own cousin to the Order? Had he no morals? He had been so concerned over her safety before — had that been real, or a con?

I stepped forward, but Ivar pressed the blade against Maude's neck and made a small slice. Maude flinched. "Go, now." Ivar warned. "The wizards want her alive, and they're on their way to meet me now. If you delay, they shall kill you both, as well."

I glanced at Iggy. Crimson blood stained the fluffy white snow he lay crumpled on. He would bleed out quickly and die, and I couldn't reach him. But if I surrendered, Maude would be taken, and abused, and used as a wicked play thing.

"Run, Bjorn. Togo, please, make him!" Maude choked out.

She was in pain — pain that ailed her daily, that was amplified when she was under stress, pain that made her bones and muscles and mind ache, pain that no soul should face without any cause. On top of that, she was bleeding, harmed by her own bloodkin, and faced the very fate she had fought so recklessly against.

I had promised her I would not let her be taken. I had promised that we would save her village.

"I know of the prophecy over the village," Ivar said sharply. "If Maude goes, the village shall be spared. She has seen this, now, as well."

Tears fell down Maude's pale cheeks. I knew that was the truth — Maude would not give into the wizards' will if it did not protect her village. And now, if she surrendered, it would save Iggy, and Togo, and I, too.

Of course, she would go in a heartbeat, and it was not fair.

Togo sheathed his katanas without a word.

I stepped forward again, gripping my sword tightly. "No! Maude! I promised you that I wouldn't let this happen —"

"She has made her choice," Togo said.

"But she hasn't! She's forced to do this — it is not her choice! Damn you!" I lunged for Ivar, but he jerked Maude in front of himself further, so if I let my sword fall, it would strike her.

I stopped inches from her outspread arms. Sobbing, Maude shielded her head — no, not shielded. She wasn't protecting herself from me. She reached out to me. Bloody hands shaking, Maude reached for me, weeping as she said again, "Run! Please! Take Iggy! They're coming!"

Togo scooped Iggy up from the bloodied snow and cradled the boy to his chest. The prince stepped forward, voice low, "Distract the man."

Distract Ivar?

Panic flooding me, I spoke quickly, "Ivar, wait! Is there any other way the wizards will not harm the village?"

"They want Maude," Ivar said. "That is all." He held the knife against her bleeding throat. "But if you stay, I am sure they can find good use for you both. After all, the Black Angel and the Manic are hard to come by, and finding you together as a pair? No one would have expected such a juicy treat." Malice laced his words and he flashed a grin. "By all means, stay, and I can be paid thrice as much!"

The prince took another step closer to me.

What was he doing?

"We'll stay," I said quickly, "just release Maude so that she is not in pain!"

Togo stood still, and Maude shook and sobbed, begging us to run. But Ivar tilted his head and then said, "Very well."

As Ivar moved to release the blade on Maude's neck, the prince lifted a hand, and white light flashed around us. The light blinded me, and white hot pain seared over my skin.

Then the light vanished, and every sense in my body dulled to nothing.

PART III

ONE

Something soft touched my face.

Bloody hands.

Tight grip.

The alley.

The men.

The voices.

Screaming, I bolted upright, swinging out a hand to defend myself.

Maude jerked backward, speaking quickly. "It's just me. I'm sorry. It's me." She knelt beside me, her clothes muddy and bloody, her wet hair clinging to her pale face. I gaped, then grabbed her in a tight hug.

"You're alive! But..." Tensing, I withdrew, glancing around at our surroundings.

We were in a small cabin. I sat on a pallet with Maude. Togo sat beside me, and Iggy slept with his head at Togo's side, bundled up in a blanket. Togo frowned at me. "He's stitched up," he said. "He should be fine."

At the little hearth, Prince Balder worked to feed the little yapping fire he must have created. He blew on the flames, and when they finally began to burn some dry logs, the prince shuffled backward. "Remove your wet clothes," he said. "I should have blankets and some tunics in the other room —"

"Where are we?" I choked, trying to stand.

The prince looked over, eyes narrow with distrust. "Away from the kingdom."

"We... we teleported," I said. "You are Gifted?"

"It is one of my Gifts," the prince said, "and if you tell a soul, I will kill you. Understood?" He looked to Togo. "You already knew?"

Togo nodded once. "It was a hunch given to me when I was hired to kill you."

The prince sighed and turned away.

"But where are we?" I demanded again. The prince's threat may be real, but I did not fear him. "We must save Maude's village — how far are we from them?"

"Not far. Norkid was west of their village, and now, we are east of the village." The prince hurried out of the room.

I stumbled after him. The cabin was musty, a layer of dust covering the dried herbs, the shelves of books and bowls on the walls, and the old wooden furniture that filled the room. The other room was right off the cabin like a mini lean-to, and boxes stood stacked to the ceiling there. The prince opened a chest, withdrawing a few pairs of old, dusty clothes, some of the fabric having holes from moths.

"Prince Balder," I whispered. "The wizards are after us —"

"I noticed," the prince huffed, tossing a dry pair of pants at me. "Thank you for saving me, though."

"Well, we —"

"I know who you both are," the prince said. "Thank you."

I dropped the topic and returned to the more urgent one at hand. "You should flee now. We'll carry on our way to the village."

"Why is the village in danger? Do the wizards need the woman so badly that they will wipe out an entire village of innocent people? That seems obnoxious, even for the Order, after the laws that have recently passed among the other kingdoms... They will put bounties on their own heads, and for what? Their ancient war?" Prince Balder clucked his tongue. "Pathetic bastards. I want them all dead. Do you?"

"Well —"

"Because if you go to the village, a war will ensue. And you are both still two men — can you truly withstand a small army of wizards?" the prince asked, turning to me, his dark eyes piercing my own.

"I understand the reality of the situation, but I must act." I nodded.

"Then the legend of the Manic is right," the prince whispered. "Once a man of war, always a man of war, is that right?"

I bowed my head, the rage burning within me yelling to release. "I am a man of God."

"I do not think those are mutually exclusive." The prince clasped my shoulder. "If you are willing to die for a village, a woman, and a child, then I shall follow you, and I shall bring my allies, as well."

"Allies?" I asked in shock. "But the people of Norkid —"

"— despise me." Prince Balder finished weakly. "Aye, they do. They are a wicked people. They are my people, however, so one day, I shall carry that cross, but for now, I shall summon my allies in other nations so that we might stand a chance against the Order. They all know the problems if the wizards gain Maude as their tool. We will not stand alone."

"You expect to gather an army in a few days?" I whispered. "Word cannot travel that fast —"

"But I can," Prince Balder flashed a grin. "Isn't it a lucky thing that the Black Angel knew of my Gift and now, I can help?"

"It is almost too good to be true," I agreed. "Is it safe for you to teleport to so many places?"

"Aye. I've trained plenty. It won't have any repercussions." The prince shrugged and withdrew more clothing before standing. "This should do it."

We took the clothing into the room. After a short while, we had all changed from our dirty, wet clothes, and huddled around the hearth in our lopsided, ill-fitting new attire. We hung the wet clothes over the furniture.

Maude sat with Iggy in her arms like a protective mother hen. The boy passed out upon changing his clothes, but his breathing and pulse remained stable for now. I wrapped Maude's neck and temple with some bandages from another wooden chest in the living room. Once everyone was warm, patched, and calm, Prince Balder set out to find canned goods in the small kitchenette off to the side of the cabin.

"I'll leave shortly," he said, "here, heat this over the fire," he shoved a few glass cans of soup at me, "and I'll go on. I should be back by nightfall."

"Even if you gather allies, it will take them days to reach the village to help us fight," Togo said, standing from the hearth. "We could still lose the village."

"We might," the prince said, his expression hardening, "but I will do all I can to ensure we don't. If the wizards are willing to ruin a village for one woman, then we shall give them a fight they never expected." Then he flashed a charming smile only a cheeky prince was capable of. "Don't be afraid now, Black Angel! After all, are we not the Black Angel, the Manic, the Gifted poet, the street rat, and the cursed prince? We're in this together! We can win!"

Togo and I exchanged a brief glance, but then I nodded with a firm smile. "Aye. Of course we shall. Creator will not forsake us now."

Even though I had no idea what Creator wanted of me, and even though nothing made sense anymore, I would not back down now. I would fight, and do whatever it took, to protect the innocent.

I looked over the room full of people. The light from the fire cast a warm glow over the people I cared for.

Creator had told me to follow Togo — and I still did not understand why, truly.

Creator had told me to save Maude — and I didn't think I was doing a good job.

Creator had told me to take Iggy along with us — and it seemed to do him more harm than good.

Creator had let us spare Prince Balder — and it, of everything, seemed to be the first thing to help us all.

But would it all be enough? Had Creator pulled us together to save the village? Or would we fail anyway?

After all, my luck wasn't good anymore, and perhaps Creator had run out of blessings to give me. But I had to do everything I could, and I could only pray Creator shed mercy on the village, even if I did not deserve it.

TWO

Prince Balder strapped his scabbard to his side and drew a dusty cloak over his shoulders, offering another smile. "Off I go. Now, you'll be safe and sound here till I return."

"If anything happens —" Maude began.

"I can return easily. Do not worry. It will be fine," the prince said with a smile. "I'll be back by nightfall, so try to have a bowl of soup warmed for me by then, yes? I'll be tired, I'm sure."

"Aye. Of course." Maude smiled at him and then focused on cooling Iggy's forehead with a damp rag.

Prince Balder frowned at me and Togo. "Try not to go stir crazy while I'm gone." And then, the young prince vanished into thin air, leaving no trace he had ever been there at all.

I exhaled heavily. "Well. We have about twelve hours to burn." I went to the hearth and stirred the soup simmering over the fire in a big iron pot.

"I'll take inventory of what's in this cabin." Togo frowned, pulling the chest of medicinal supplies closer to Maude. "First, let's wake the boy, and give him some medicine for his fever. We can't afford to find a healer until the allies come."

Iggy needed to fight until then.

Twelve hours, or more, suddenly seemed even longer.

"Aye," Maude said, and she gently woke Iggy enough for Togo to force some black liquid down his throat. Iggy coughed, but passed out again.

We remained silent so the boy could rest. Togo investigated the cabin, looking over every crate, box, and cabinet or cupboard in the tiny, dusty place. I kept the fire burning and looked beyond the thick curtains every so often, but I saw nothing but snow falling down.

The snow would make travel difficult. Would it delay us greatly? Would the prince's banding together make any difference? Surely, he couldn't teleport our army to the village — we would need to travel. But if the snow continued...

After a few hours, I made more soup, and we ate around the fire. Iggy slept soundly. His fever had broken, but we didn't try to wake him yet.

Maude forced half a bowl of soup down before she sat it aside with shaky hands. "I'm sorry," she said. Her hair hung around her face and her shoulders slumped.

"You have nothing to apologize for," I said firmly. "Nothing at all."

"This is —"

"Not your fault." Togo finished simply. And then, he changed the subject. "We'll have to travel to the village as soon as the allies are prepared. But I am not sure if it is wise for you to accompany us," he said to Maude.

"I have to." Maude paled. "It's my village —"

"And the wizards want you," Togo said. "If you are there, then our forces will be divided between defending the people and defending you."

Maude flinched and looked down at her hands. "I see. But... But I could help..."

"You have very little skill with a blade," Togo continued, "and besides, can you kill another man?"

Maude sat up stiffly, her eyes flashing. "I can do whatever it takes to protect my village!"

"Perhaps. But there are too many risks. I think you should remain here," Togo said. "Iggy won't recover in time, so you should tend to him."

I grimaced, but said nothing. I agreed with Togo. But it must feel humiliating to be in Maude's position, and I did not want to hurt her.

"You expect me to stay here? After all of this?" Maude whispered. Tears rolled down her ashen face.

I cringed. "Maude —"

"It is safest for you, and for the allies willing to fight for you and against the wizards," Togo said. "After the battle, you should then pursue a fellowship with one of the Gifted alliances. But if you are taken amid the fight, there is no future."

There is no future. Did he have to put it so harshly? Then again, he was right. I rubbed my face. "Maude, I think it's best, but if you choose to come, then we won't stop you, either. It is your decision."

Maude kept her head low. The crackle of the fire filled the little room. After a long moment, Maude said, her voice strained and small, "If you both think I should stay, then I shall. I trust you. But…"

"None of this is your fault, or your burden to bear alone." I stopped her. "And none of us are being forced to help — these wizards are not only after you, so we must stop them."

Togo nodded.

"Aye." Maude said nothing more. She wiped her tears quickly and watched the fire.

Guilt ate my gut. I wanted to comfort her, to say something to lift her spirits, but I didn't want to be disrespectful, either, and intrude on her silence. So after a long moment, I said softly, "I do not think Creator has brought us this far to forsake us now… I do not think He would be angry if you are wise about these next steps in our journey. And I do not think He wants you harmed, either."

Maude tensed as if I had prodded her with a red-hot iron. She glanced up, tears shimmering in her eyes again. "Aye... I... I suppose He doesn't."

Did she believe that? When she was in pain daily, when she was weak and broken because of some invisible ailment in her body — did she truly believe that Creator cared for, and did not wish her harm? I wanted her to believe in that love. But how could I? It was her revelation to find, and I only prayed she had just found it.

Reaching over, I patted her shoulder gently. "Rest, now."

Maude curled up nearby Iggy. Without a word, Togo tossed a blanket over her.

"Thank you, Togo," Maude murmured before falling asleep.

I smiled softly and eyed Togo. In the beginning, he had admired Maude for her strength — but even after realizing her strength was not all she was, he still was willing to put his life on the line for her with me. I had forced him to help us at first... but I don't think we were forcing him anymore, and I don't think, either, that we were only with Togo to repay our debt anymore.

Sitting in that little cabin, near the warmth of the fire, the three of us were more than a debtor and debtees, and more than even partners.

Dare I say it, Creator, but I think this might be what a family looks like, isn't it?

THREE

By nightfall, Prince Balder returned. He appeared in the center of the living room, his cloak hanging down, with an exhausted smile on his dimpled face. "I'm not late, am I?" he asked.

"Right on time," I said, stepping over to take his cloak. "How did it go?" "You are a very impatient priest," Prince Balder mused, shaking some snowflakes from his curly blond hair. "May I at least have that soup I was promised?"

"We're running out of time," Togo said from where he sat at the window, keeping watch and smoking his pipe.

Maude stirred the soup over the fire. She had tied her hair up, and looked a little better since waking from her nap an hour earlier. "Here," she said. "Sit down."

Prince Balder blushed slightly but sat at the table quickly. "Thank you, Miss Maude."

Maude frowned a little at the title, but didn't correct the prince, and she sat the bowl of soup in front of him. She sat without another word.

I sat at the table beside Maude. "Did it go well?" That seemed like a simple enough question to answer.

"Aye, very well," the prince said. "As it turns out, none of the other nations wanted me dead." He said it with such a jolly smile, it almost erased the fact that only his father had wanted his head. "And they're all aware that the wizards have been fervently seeking more Gifted to join their ranks. When I explained the situation, they all agreed that the wizards must be stopped immediately. If they were to capture Maude, well, things could take a very quick, dire turn, and since most of the nations have been at peace for so long, no one is interested in another outbreak of the Order." As the prince spoke, he devoured his bowl of soup.

Togo frowned. "So what allies are we counting on?"

"Well, to begin with, our closest ally is Buacach. They can reach us in a week, and Creator appears to be on our side, because one of their Gifted soldiers is able to control the wind —"

"He is going to move the snow?" Togo asked.

"Aye, she will divert the winter snowfall. It still puts the Buacach Fellowship at a narrow arrival as to when the wizards are presumably going to attack, but it is close." The prince nodded.

"Why can't you teleport everyone here?" I asked. "Over the span of a few days, shouldn't you be able to transfer a reasonable army here? At least, enough Gifted to defend the village, in case the wizards arrive sooner than we anticipated?"

"Aye, I shall," Balder said. "But I shall be teleporting Gifted from Farsik, actually — there is a squad of highly trained individuals there willing to come to our aid. They're hoping to take a good portion of wizards as prisoners."

I tensed a bit at that, but nodded. "And the squad will defend the village in the meantime while we wait for Buacach's forces?"

"That's the plan." Balder nodded tiredly and finished the mug of mead. "Of course, I can transfer as many as I can, but I am not strong enough to teleport armies of men within a few days, and if I am too exhausted before the fight, I won't be much help, and I do think my Gift can be valuable in battle."

"Of course," I said. "We don't want to break you."

Prince Balder laughed, slapping my arm. "Do not worry about that! I am in the prime of my youth. A battle like this is what I've waited for in my life. It will prove to the nations that I am truly fit to be king. When this is over, when I've fulfilled my promise to my four soldiers, then I can return and do justice to Norkid!" The passion in his voice made the hair on my neck stand on end. He believed every bit of what he said. I had never met a young man so dedicated to a cause before.

"Creator bless you," I agreed, "let it be done."

Balder lifted his mug of mead. I hit it with my own mug, and Balder said, "For the glory of the kingdom! Let Creator's face shine upon us in our endeavor!"

Togo lifted his pipe slightly as we toasted to the decree. Maude sipped her drink quietly, and Balder and I continued our discussion of plans, details, and the like. While the entire journey ahead was uncertain, I finally felt as if

Creator truly did hear us, and He would be with us, no matter the sins of my past.

Perhaps, by the end of this mission, I could be free.

Free from the memories, the nightmares, the blood on my hands, the fear that while I had prayed to be a new man in Creator, that I still was rejected and was not enough — but perhaps, it could all be left behind.

Or was that a naive dream meant for young men, and not for men battered by life and reality, and the truth that no man could truly be washed anew, and that the Letters missexplained such a thing?

FOUR

OVER THE NEXT FEW days, time moved like a falling star. Prince Balder teleported a Farsik squad of men to the village's edge. Togo and I were teleported to the squad's camp after they were arranged, though Balder stayed at the cabin with Maude after he teleported us promptly.

I disliked the feeling of being teleported, but it was a miraculous way of getting around, though we couldn't overdo it, and thus, would not see the village's edge again until the final battle.

The Farsiks were large men, with dark skin, heavy eyes, and they moved with expertise and confidence. Their leader, a man called Om, greeted Togo and I at the little camp's edge. They had chosen the side of a creek, at a cave's mouth, with a clear exit into the forest so that they could not be backed into any corner, nor could they be attacked from above. The keen awareness of their surroundings made me shiver slightly.

"Togo and Priest Bjorn," Om said, "it is an honor to meet you after hearing all Prince Balder has said."

Prince Balder had left as soon as he teleported us and introduced us to the leader. I almost wished he had stayed. Then again, what did I have to fear? Om was on our side. And he did not know my true identity, or Togo's, did he?

Togo nodded silently, and I said, "It's an honor to meet you, Om... Truly... Your alliance is a blessing. We shall not fail any of you."

Om flashed a bright, pearly grin. "We shall not fail, brother. Creator will give us the strength to crush these serpents under foot." He gestured toward his squad of men standing at attention. "Let us show you the camp and what we have scouted so far, so that when the time arrives, you two can also fight with wisdom."

I nodded, and Togo and I joined the Farsik squad.

When we returned to the cabin, Prince Balder sprawled out on a pallet, sighing heavily. "Teleportation is a tiresome thing."

"Thank you," I said, "I think we are fully prepared now. The squad is highly skilled — even if the Buacach forces are delayed, I think we would still stand a good chance against wizards." My stomach growled as the smell of stew hit my nostrils.

Maude stood near the fire, stirring boiling stew in the giant pot. I peered over her shoulder. "That smells wonderful."

"Thank you, but it isn't quite my doing." Maude nodded toward the cupboard of canned foods.

Prince Balder laughed softly. "My mentor was a hearty cook. He canned often, however, because I am not, and would have starved during our hunts if he had not left me something edible to eat while he was out."

The prince had not mentioned his mentor, besides when he told me that the sword he carried was the only heirloom he had from the man. "He sounds like he was a good man," I said softly.

"He was the best." Prince Balder turned his face to watch Maude cook, his smile gone. "Anyway, I apologize for my complaints."

"You should," Iggy piped up from his corner near the fire. He was whittling a stick. Feeling much better, his attitude had returned and doubled. "Complaining is for wussies."

"Language," Maude said.

Iggy rolled his eyes.

It was impossible to tame a street rat, but I smiled at Maude's attempt.

We ate in silence. There was no reason to discuss what we had learned — Maude knew her village, and the word that the squad was skilled was enough to give a slight relief for her. Besides, Iggy wouldn't be coming with us, so he didn't need to know about the situation.

Still, the silence gnawed at my gut. I was used to Maude's tales. I was used to joking and irritating Togo.

Time had slowed, and it ticked by mercilessly, leaving us plenty of ability to create scenarios in our minds that could drive us insane before the battle even began. Time was the true decider of the fate of a war. And I could only pray it would be on our side.

After dinner, I cleaned up the kitchen with Maude. Iggy fell asleep on his pallet after harping at Prince Balder for stories — but Balder didn't give in to telling any grand tales tonight, so Iggy passed out near the fire. Balder fell asleep shortly after.

Togo lit his pipe, taking his guard beside the window. I sat at the table tiredly with a mug of coffee.

Maude sat too, fiddling with her hands nervously. "Did... did the village look... all right?"

"It looked all right," I said. "We didn't get close, though, so I don't know any details. I apologize."

"That's enough. Thank you." She nodded and crossed her arms on the table, dropping her head.

"You should not weaken yourself by worrying," Togo chastened.

"I know." Maude nodded again. "I'm praying more than I have in my life, and I can only hope Creator listens. If... if His will is not my will, then, so be it, and we'll... handle whatever that might be..."

Still, it was terrifying to have your entire village hanging in some invisible balance between life and death. It must have felt even worse knowing there was nothing Maude could do. Doubtlessly, also, she still struggled with guilt — but this ordeal was not her fault. It was the Order's fault.

Creator, give Maude peace. And guide our hands for the war ahead.

Sipping my coffee, I said, "Get some rest, yes?"

Maude hesitated, glancing up at me.

Ah. There it was. The question dancing behind her heavy eyes. The question she had not asked for days.

"Bjorn?" Maude whispered.

"Aye?"

"Prince Balder called you..."

"The Manic," I said quietly.

"Aye. Is it true?"

I put my coffee down, holding Maude's gaze. "Yes. It is true."

"I have heard of the Manic in passing." Maude gulped, but instead of looking away or turning ghoulish, she said, "Creator has saved you from the darkness, then. I'm grateful." She squeezed my forearm gently. "Thank you for saving me and my people."

"I'll do my best. I believe most of the saving will be done by the squad," I said, trying to keep my tone light. My insides jumbled.

Maude knew who I was — and she did not care? Or perhaps she didn't know who the Manic truly was?

No one in Norkid, or the surrounding areas, could be clueless as to the reality of who the Manic had been. Maude knew my deepest secret now, and she had not fled.

Nor had Togo, though, he had known all along, hadn't he?

Maude stood then, and gave me a brief hug around the neck. "Thank you." Her voice was firm. She did not want me to brush off her words — so I didn't, and forced a weak nod, and patted her arm.

Maude stepped over to Togo, and without hesitation, she hugged his neck, too, smiling. "Thank you, Togo. I know we still owe you much, but when this is over, I'll still follow you both anywhere."

Togo didn't return her hug, but he said, "I suppose we could endure that."

Maude smiled and went to tidy up in the other room.

My heart lodged in my throat. When this was over...

Would we make it? Would there be a life for us after this? Could there be?

Or would Creator demand my life? Togo's life? Or, no, Creator forbid, the others' lives? Maude could not be harmed, her village could not be harmed, and I had to protect Iggy, too — would Creator take them from me?

He had taken so much already...

I pushed the fears aside.

Creator takes nothing. Things are lost, but Creator is not the monster seeking to ruin me. I mustn't think such.

I glanced at Togo, but he didn't look at me, so I said nothing. Maude returned and laid down in her pallet, falling asleep promptly. I sat up for a few hours with Togo, lost in prayer. The fire burned and its warm light flooded the room. I finished my coffee eventually after it went cold, and my fervent, fearful prayers reminded me of the ones in the Letters.

I could not help but pray the Creator saw my fear as not faithless, but as human, and that was why I needed Him.

FIVE

Togo woke me in the middle of the night with a touch and a whisper. "It's time to go to the village. The wizards are there."

I bolted upright, but before I could question him, I spotted Maude standing behind him. Her pale face and wringing hands let me know that she must have had another vision and told Togo of it.

That was all the word we needed, then.

I dressed hastily while Togo woke Prince Balder from his heavy slumber. The prince yanked his belt and scabbard on, mumbling, "Will you be all right here alone with Iggy, Maude?"

"Aye." Maude nodded, still standing near the hearth. She shook hard. I wondered what she had seen in her vision. Had it scared her so greatly? Or was she only afraid of what she did not know? Still, now was no time to ask. And it was not my place to question the visions or future, anyway.

It was time for war.

Togo stood ready, dressed and armed, and I stepped over to Maude. "Be alert," I said. "And take heart." I hugged Maude briefly before going to Togo's side.

Prince Balder moved toward us, voice low. "Ready?"

Before he could touch us and begin the teleportation, Iggy jumped up from his pallet and tackled the three of us in a hug. He was small, but his grip was tight. "Be safe," he said sharply, "and hurry back."

I ruffled his hair and Prince Balder flashed a smile and saluted the boy. "Aye, aye, Captain Iggy."

With that, the prince grasped Togo and I by our arms, and we vanished from the little cozy cabin.

The Manic, the Black Angel, and the prince of Norkid arrived at the village of Raymorn while the moon hung high and smoke billowed from the small cabins.

Prince Balder had teleported us to the edge of a nearby mountain to take in the surrounding area briefly.

The village lay under siege. A small group of wizards walked through the little town as if they were untouchable — red magic burst from their hands and wrecked the buildings, one by one, as flames lapped up the debris. Men raced to take up arms against the enemy while women and children ran for the trees.

Were we too late?

Surely not.

The squad of Farsik Gifted surrounded the wizards — I spotted them from the edge of the mountain, but the wizards hadn't noticed the ambush yet. We still had time to engage.

"Let's go." Balder grabbed us again, and we appeared in the middle of the village then.

Togo dove into the action without hesitation. He wielded his katanas with lethal grace, and in seconds, had killed one of the wizards approaching from the footpath ahead. The corpse, in two pieces, fell with dull thuds under the veil of night.

In the clamor of the raging fight, I ran.

Three wizards stood on the path ahead of me. One shot magic into a cabin, and the other two used their powers to capture a woman and child. Red magic wove around the woman as she screamed and held her baby tighter — the magic could squeeze the life from them, or throw them into the woods with lethal force. The wizards had their lives in their own hands and would not hesitate to end them.

I ran into them.

The white hot rage took over, and the Gift that I had buried for so long returned.

SIX

White hot rage encompassed me. Every fiber of my being screamed with strength and bloodlust.

I tackled the two wizards to the ground, and with fire burning from my hands, I tore into their throats like a bear might rip apart a fox. Dead within seconds, the wizards fell limp under my bloody, fiery hands, and their magic ceased.

The woman screamed again. Her eyes, wide with fear, met mine, and then she turned with her child and ran from me.

I turned to the third wizard that had set the cabin ablaze. Yelling, I charged him, my fire still racing up my arms. The wizard lifted his left hand and a wall of red magic slammed against me. It threw me off my feet and took the air from my lungs.

Snarling, I stood again, and prayed under my breath. "Shield me, Creator. Guide my hands and let my enemies fall!"

The words pierced the pandemonium around me: men cried, blades against blades rang out, and fires roared as more cabins went up in flames. The Farsiks and villagers fought hard around us — but the wizards grew in number. Were they teleporting more men in?

The wizard before me laughed softly. "Worried, Priest?" He spat. "Your prayer sounds desperate to me." He lifted another red wall of magic. It looked impenetrable, but I knew better.

I ran into the wall of red and throttled the wizard before he knew what happened. He fell on his back, and I pinned him to the ground.

Pure fear contorted the man's face. He lifted his hands to shield his head, but was too late.

My fists and fire became one, and I killed the wizard with a sharp snap of his neck. The stench of burned flesh filled my nostrils.

I fought as the Manic, and time went still.

White hot rage.

Fiery red power erupted from my core and danced on my hands.

I tore into man after man, leaving bodies trailing behind me as I progressed into the little village.

This was who I was.

Manic.

This was what I was.

Manic.

A yell came from deep within me as I ripped apart a magician that stood over a fallen villager. The man lay contorted, his body mangled from a strong magic, his empty eyes staring into the dark sky above.

This village was innocent. The people deserved life — and I would gladly lose myself to the Manic if it ensured their safety.

If this means Maude may live, I will die as a monster, Creator.

The wizard dropped dead as I released his broken neck. I ran onward, the zeal burning in my body unlike I had ever felt before.

Was I human?

Was I Creator's? Was I a new being in His image?

Or was I Manic? Was I a monster made for war, made of blood and death?

Or perhaps, was I all of those things at once, and could a man be many spirits or souls, or could he be a very broken soul of many pieces?

What was I?

Then again, in this moment, it did not matter.

Another wizard tackled me. He sent a bolt of green magic into my face to briefly blind me, but I laughed and sneered. I gripped the man's neck hard. He screamed in surprise.

It did not matter if this night I sealed my fate as a monster that could never see the light of Creator again, because tonight, I protected the ones I loved, and I would not fear Creator's fate for me. So long as Maude, Togo, Iggy, and Balder lived, I would gladly be damned forever.

"Bjorn!" a voice called through the chaos.

In the middle of the village, Prince Balder battled two wizards. The prince wielded his sword expertly, but the magicians held the upper hand. One sent a bolt of blue magic into Balder's shoulder, and he cried out, his sword falling from his grip.

I lunged forward. "Togo!" I wouldn't make it in time — but if Togo was close by, he could give us a square fight.

Something black flashed in the glow of the burning cabins.

Togo rushed forward and cut down one of the wizards from behind. His katanas moved like extensions of his arms, and the wizard fell dead. The second wizard grabbed Balder, but before he could give the final blow, I tackled them to the ground.

Fire-engulfed hands wrapping around the wizard's neck, I screamed a cry that burned from deep within. The wizard's magic battled against me — blue waves of electricity bounced into my chest. The pain seared, but I laughed. The stronger the magic attacked me, the louder my laugh grew.

The wizard writhed beneath me. "Manic!" he cried. "Join us!" His dazzling green eyes lit up with admiration. "Join us, and be your own god!"

My fire burned the man's skin. It ate into his flesh. And still, he grinned up at me, sweat pouring from his temples. "Become one with us, Manic!" he begged fervently, like a lost man that had found his creator.

The white, hot rage, the Manic, the Gift — ached within me, and subsided.

My hands faltered. My fire died.

I held the man by his singed neck. He would die — unless a healer found him. And still, he looked at me as if I were god himself.

"Creator, forgive me!" I choked. Then I snatched the wizard upright. "Repent! Repent!" I clasped his bleeding face. "Repent! Please! Forgive me!"

Laughter erupted from the wizard's mangled throat. "Your god is not here! Become a god or be lost — that is your fate!" He gestured toward the burning village around us. Embers danced in the night sky above.

Tears ran down my face. I shook the wizard. "Repent! Stop this madness!"

But before I could plead further, a small dagger flew and lodged into the wizard's skull. He went limp in my hands.

I jerked upright.

"Fight or leave," Togo said sharply from behind me, and then he ran off to fight alongside the Farsik soldiers.

A sob choked me, but I stumbled after Togo.

I was willing to be damned to hell if it meant saving my loved ones — but I had not expected to meet souls on this battlefield. I had expected to meet enemies so far gone into the darkness that they would be easily killed.

But I had been one of those souls, so lost in the darkness... And had Creator not dragged me from the depths and given me light?

How could I kill these wizards and damn them for eternity?

But if I let them live... They would kill innocents.

A scream of rage tore from my lungs. I entered the battle again without hesitation.

SEVEN

The Farsiks and villagers fought mercilessly in the little village. The Gifted Farsiks pushed the remaining wizards to one side of the battlefield. Now, all of the living women and children had vanished. Bodies of villagers and wizards covered the village, and every burning building began to crumble.

It was not over — but what good had we really done?

Blood pouring from my temples, I followed the Farsik men. Togo battled a lone wizard to my left, but I pressed on.

Prince Balder worked alongside the Farsiks, but his footing stumbled. While the Gifted worked in tight formation now, Balder staggered sideways as a wizard lured him away from our group.

"Balder!" I yelled. "Get back!"

If we were gaining the upper hand, then the wizards would divide our forces and pick us off. Balder was the weakest link.

Balder dodged the wizard's powerful magic. I raced toward them, but the wizard sent another bolt of red magic, and it slammed Balder in the chest. He dropped backward, blood spurting from his mouth.

I got between them and tackled the wizard before he could defend himself. My fiery Gift exploded from my hands and engulfed the wizard's head. He fell dead, and I jumped upright again. "Balder, fall back!"

Balder didn't stand. Blood spilled from his mouth, and he rolled onto his hands and knees. His sword lay nearby.

He's in worse shape than I thought, I realized. I grabbed the prince and hauled him to his feet. "Go back," I said, "I'll send the healer —"

"It's Togo," the prince choked.

"What?" I dragged him a few steps, trying to scan the village for a safe place to drop him until a healer could fix him.

"Togo is the mercenary after Maude — th-this is just a distraction," Balder said, before coughing up more blood. "I-I heard them —"

I dropped the prince against one of the few cabins that wasn't in flames, out of sight of the Farsiks and wizards fighting at the edge of the village. "Stop talking nonsense and focus on living until I fetch help —"

"Togo is going to betray you," the prince cried. "He saved you both only to take Maude to the wizards himself!"

A loud, ear-ringing *boom* came from the edge of the town, and blackness covered the world.

EIGHT

I moved.

Even in the darkness, I moved.

Even with ash and embers and rubble falling around me, I moved.

Even with blood pouring down my face, and my fire raging through my body and burning in my fists, I moved.

I moved into the darkness, without fear, without knowing where my feet fell, but it didn't matter, because someplace in the darkness was Togo. I had to reach him.

Cries and screams echoed in the dark. It was a thick, heavy darkness — magic, no doubt. The wizards probably created some sort of spell so they could fight the soldiers under the cover. The Gifted Farsiks and remaining villagers would be pummeled if they fought blindly — anyone would be.

I need to join the fight, a part of my spirit pleaded.

But the other part begged, *Find Togo first.*

I stumbled onward, ears still ringing from the blast. Had it been some sonic blast of magic that caused the darkness to fall? The sky was gone now. The darkness almost physically pushed against me as I moved. It wouldn't be easy to fight in — but we would have to find a way to defeat it.

"Togo!" I called. Or, I tried to call. I could hardly hear my own voice among the cries of the battling men far behind me, at the village's edge.

Lungs searing with pain, I took a few more steps. My left hand stretched out and I hit a wall — a cabin. I stepped around it. "Togo!"

Up ahead, in the dark, I heard heavy breathing. I moved toward it. "Togo!" I almost hardly recognized the sound — Togo didn't get out of breath during fights very often. But tonight's battle had even the Black Angel at his limits.

"They're winning," Togo said, voice hoarse. "We need to hurry —"

"Balder heard you speaking with the wizards," I panted. "Is it true?"

"What?" Togo stood inches from me. I felt the heat from his body, smelled the blood that no doubt stained every inch of his body.

"You were hired to turn me and Maude into the Order. Is it true?" I demanded, hands shaking, and the fire erupted on my fists then.

The little light illuminated Togo's form before me. He stood with a slight lean, as if his left leg were injured, and blood covered his face and clothes. His eyes, usually guarded, or empty, practically screamed.

"It's true," I said.

"I was hired," Togo said, voice low, "but I did not bring either of you to the Order, and I told them tonight I was their enemy."

Rage burst within me. White hot rage. I lunged, fire still on my hands, but Togo sidestepped me.

"Traitor," I snarled, swinging at him again. "You're going to give us over to them! How could you do that to Maude?" She had done nothing to anyone. Her own bloodkin had betrayed her. And she had fought to help Togo, even. Blast it all — she wouldn't have crossed paths with the man if it hadn't been for me. But if Togo had been hired, that wasn't true, though — he would have found us both whether I initiated anything or not.

Togo stepped forward. "I am fighting at your side and I am defending Maude and her village," he said sharply. "If I were on their side now, no one would have known, and you would both be in the hands of the Order." He said it with such simplicity. I knew it was true. The Black Angel was as good as the Manic. And we never failed a job.

"Why didn't you tell me?" I demanded.

"It would have endangered you further, and did I not tell you to run when I met you?" Togo snapped. "Don't ask dumb questions. Let's go back to the fight —"

The darkness grew heavier, and the light in my hands flickered slightly. I tensed as the magic around us grew denser, making it harder to breathe, and I tried to keep the Gift going.

Togo's eyes darted beyond me. "Bjorn!"

And then everything went black again. The last thing I saw was Togo reaching out for me, utter rage and panic in his eyes, before cold, searing pain flooded my skull.

PART IV

ONE

I WOKE IN A small, musty cell, and I felt my way around for a moment to identify rock, more rock, and some more wet rock, and then a row of metal bars. I was in some sort of stone cell, then — but I had no clue where.

I could safely assume the wizards had taken me: that must have been what Togo had tried protecting me from. And since wizards could teleport others, also, I could be in another continent, or in the Bour Mountains.

I felt my head. The blood was dried, and the gashes had all stopped bleeding by now, so it had been at least a couple of hours since I had been left here. I wasn't starving or anything, so it hadn't been too long, I assumed.

Stomach twisting, I took a weak breath, and knelt on the cold rocks. The cell had no light, and there was nothing beyond the cell bars.

I was alone.

Maude was gone. Possibly taken, too, if the Farsiks and civilians had lost to the wizards. Was she here? Someplace? Would Iggy be with her?

I took a shaky breath and whispered her name, but in the cold darkness, nothing replied.

I rubbed my face. Balder was probably dead, if the healer never found him in that dense darkness.

And Togo was gone, too, probably for good, since I was in the Order's hands now.

I pressed my forehead to the stone floor, exhaled weakly, and prayed. "Creator, You are holy, and beautiful, and kind. I thank You for all you have done — without Your grace, nothing would exist. And that alone is enough to cause the world to praise You, and only You." My hands shook. "I have one thing to ask." My insides trembled. I had never felt such fear before — not fear for myself, but fear for people I genuinely loved. Had I ever loved another before? I could not say I had. Ever.

"Please, let Maude and Iggy be free and safe. Please." And mentally, I added, *please let the Gifted association in*

Buacach have reached them all by now, so that Maude can join their forces, and live without fear or manipulation. And please, Creator, let Iggy find a family too, and live as normal of a life as a street rat possibly could.

Tears burned my eyes.

That was the truth, wasn't it?

I loved them.

I, Mabuz the Manic, the killer, the Gifted beast of legend that slaughtered countless men on the battlefield, that had served the Order before, that had tried to leave his old life of blood behind, had surrendered my broken soul to Creator, and had loved four souls more than my own, and now I had lost them.

Was this how Creator finally punished me? Had Creator saved me, blessed me, led me, only to take away my family now?

What lesson did I need to learn? What did Creator expect from me now? What was the right decision here?

Desperation rose in my chest.

I didn't know.

I did not know what Creator expected from me. Was this a test? A punishment? Or a sick twist of fate that Creator had simply allowed?

Creator, I prayed silently. My heart and soul wept where only Creator could hear — if He cared enough to listen. *Am I not saved? All I have thought and prayed and lived by — I did not doubt You for a moment, but what do I do now? Was I wrong to think I could be a light? Is this Your way of punishing me? Is this my fate — to lose the only ones I have ever loved?*

I don't understand it! You told me to join Togo. I remember. You told me to save Maude. I remember. And you led us to save Iggy and Balder, as well. I did not act on my own will — You ordained each of these relationships! So why take them from me?

The tears ran down my bloody face and filled my beard. I wept bitterly. "Creator, why?"

I had no misheard, had I?

Was this all my doing?

Had I made things worse?

Doubts and fears clouded my mind. I tried to sort them out, I tried to pray, I tried to remain calm — but I had never been in any sort of situation while my heart loved another, and it consumed me.

I would be tortured. Whether for information or coercion, I would be tortured by the wizards until I gave in. But I did not fear that. I had been tortured before, plenty of times, and in plenty of wicked ways. There was nothing a man could do to break my body or mind because both had already been broken at one time, and repeating the process did not scare me.

However, I had never been tortured while my heart had known love.

Already, the love burned and raged and screamed within me.

I did not wish to die here — to die for the light was a worthy cause, of course, but I wished to see Maude, and Togo, and Iggy, and Balder again. But I would never see them again. Because I would never ally with the Order. So the wizards would have to kill me, or I would have to feign alliance, and kill myself at first chance. Either way, I would never see my family again, nor would I be able to protect them as I had promised.

My spirit twisted like a beast tore my insides.

I took another breath and finished my prayer. "Spare them, Creator. Take me. But spare them." I was no one to request such things — but the Letters told us to ask Creator, and not to shy from His face. I might be doomed, I might be wrong about everything, but I would still try to follow the commands so that the others could be saved.

After all, I had nothing to lose.

And deep down, I still believed Creator loved me.

Even if He was breaking me apart.

Beyond the cell doors, metal creaked and keys jangled. A light came from a door I had not seen, illuminating a very small, narrow corridor that led to my little cell.

In the light, a tall man stood. A long, black cloak hung over his broad shoulders, and he held a golden staff in his left hand and a small, glowing lantern in his right.

My blood ran cold.

"Hello, Manic. Or do you still insist on Priest Bjorn?" The man chuckled. "*Bjorn*, then, if it pleases you — how do you feel? You took quite the beating. Apparently, your Gift, and your holy divine protection," he spoke the words with malice, "allowed you to fight like the berserker you were once known as. Still, you were injured, so I imagine you shall take quite some time to heal."

I didn't respond, watching him closely as he approached. He stopped outside of my cell.

"I heard you praying, yes?" the wizard asked. "I'm sorry to say, but Maude was killed during the operation — she put up quite a fight, but she ended her own life before we could enslave her." His eyes narrowed in the dim light from the lantern.

The wizard's words rang in my head. My blood ran cold. I rejected them.

"You are lying to break my mind and spirit," I said calmly. "A tactic I have used before on many men." A man, in the clutches of the enemy, would believe many terrible things, and would wear down quickly if he thought all was lost beyond his cell doors.

"It would sound so," the wizard said, "but when faced with the reality that Maude would be used to harm another, she took her own life to ensure that never happened. It is unfortunate — but if we cannot have her, we can always wait for the next highly Gifted... In the meantime, you shall work alongside us again."

Panic settled in my gut, but I fought it hard. Maude wasn't dead — this was just the wizard's attempt of breaking me down.

But Maude wouldn't let herself be taken...

It made sense that she would have killed herself before the Order could enslave her...

But... No.

She had to be alive. And I had no way of knowing if the Order had her and lied to me, or if she had somehow escaped — had Balder lived, and teleported Togo back to her to shield her? Or had the Gifted Buacach army found her and defended her and Iggy?

I had no way of knowing a damn thing, and everything burdened my chest like molten iron filling me up from the inside.

"Do you agree, Manic?" the wizard asked, switching my name, doubtlessly on purpose — another thorn in my side to wear me down.

After all, from the man's perspective, nothing held me back from rejoining the Order now.

I had left to be free... but what had freedom done for me?

I had still resorted to violence and killing. I had still shed blood.

And the few people I had cared for?

Maude and Iggy and Balder were gone — and if they had somehow survived, they were still far from me, and endangered, and possibly doomed.

Togo was going to betray me — and if he had changed his mind about that, he still had not told me the truth upfront, either.

I had nothing out there.

I had no future, no family, no love, no freedom.

Creator, why have You forsaken me? I have tried to be your humble servant, I have followed Your will even when I did not understand — was it all a sham? Was it all for nothing?

Heart in my chest, I whispered, with tears rolling down my bloody cheeks, with the darkness to my back, and the lantern glowing warmly before me, for all of the world to hear, even Creator himself: "I will die before I join the dark again. I am a new soul, created by Creator, and I choose the light, even if it slays me."

TWO

Chains were locked around my wrists. If I used my Gift, I could melt them off — but the wizard sighed and stepped back. "You cannot melt this metal. We learned our lesson last time."

I eyed him sharply. He had hung the lantern up on the stone wall and chained me to the ground: I knew what came next, especially if the wizards had gone out of their way to find a metal that I could not escape from.

"If you do not accept our alliance willingly, we shall only enforce it." He nodded, then reached over and grabbed my chin tightly. "What did Togo tell you?"

I bristled, but looked the wizard in the eyes and spat in his face.

Snarling, the man wiped his face and hissed, "What did he tell you in the veil?"

The veil. Was that what they called the great darkness that had covered the village before I was attacked from behind and blacked out? I gritted my teeth, remaining silent. Why had they cast that veil? And why did this wizard want to know about what Togo had told me?

He stepped back and tied his long, black hair up. It reminded me of Togo's hair, but it was longer than Togo's. "I'm asking a simple question."

"Aha. But I'm just a dumb priest," I said. "I'm just the brawny Manic. You hit me too hard in the village earlier. I can't think straight. I must have lost my memory." I flashed a crooked grin.

The wizard slapped me hard. "You're as cocky as ever. It's unbecoming, especially for a supposed man of Creator."

"What do you care about how Creator's followers act?" I laughed. "You follow Abaddon, and kill innocent women and children. There is nothing as disgusting as that."

"You followed him, too," the man said softly, "you think any god can erase what you did while serving Abaddon?"

A strange, hot resolve settled over me. "I do," I said. "Creator has washed away the blood from my hands and I am made as pure snow. The Letters say so." Even if I struggled to believe such a thing, in the heat of a battle, or when I was forsaken in a dungeon, I knew it was still true.

Truth did not have to change a person's emotions, or fears, or trials, to remain the truth.

The man laughed and released my face again, stepping backward. "Very well. I shall drag the answers from you by force, then. Togo was a fool to make you his ally."

Despite the obvious threat from the wizard, I felt a surge of relief.

Togo considered me an ally?

How could this wizard know that?

And why did I hope it was true?

"Why would you know that?" I asked tightly. "Togo betrayed us. You bastards hired him to bring Maude and I into the Order."

"Yet, he fought us," the wizard seethed. "And in front of you, even! I had hoped that I would be able to fool you, but the piece of shit made it quite clear what side he chose, didn't he? No matter, is it, really? You'll join us, even if he won't."

What did he mean — had Togo not joined the Order? Had they only hired him for the one job of bringing us in? If that were true, then why was the wizard so pissed about everything? Wizards didn't take much personally. A mercenary going rogue shouldn't have this man demanding me for information.

My mind reeled. So what then?

The wizard told me to kneel. I barely heard him. He hit me again, and I laughed. "Whatever torture you have intended, I've already had," I said smugly. "But by all means, whatever helps you get off."

The wizard sent a strong blast of red magic into my chest, knocking the wind out of me, sending every nerve in my body screaming in agony. Vision blackening, I didn't make a sound. If the bastard wanted to get information out of me, he could play hell trying. Because if Maude was dead, and Balder, and if Iggy was with the village, and if Togo had left us, then why would I want to make it out alive, or bring harm to Togo?

Another blast of magic struck me. It was unlike any magic I had felt before — the wizard was greatly skilled, but he was still holding back, since our session had only started.

This blast of magic settled deep within my chest. It seared through every fiber of my lungs, like a thousand tiny blades ripped through the organ. Unable to breathe, I struggled to remain standing.

The wizard reached out and kicked my left knee out from beneath me. I dropped and hit the stone floor hard, but still couldn't draw a breath as the magic pierced my lungs. The searing pain became cold — like shards of ice prickling my lungs — until it slowly dulled. I gulped in a breath and burst into laughter.

I flashed a grin, laughing like the Manic I truly was. "Is that all you have, pretty wizard boy?"

THREE

Hours upon hours stacked up, and the torture grew predictable, though torture usually was mundane and methodical. Every so often, you had a madman handle the matter, and he might make hasty or passionate decisions, but usually, men in the line of torture work wanted answers, and knew the methods behind getting what they needed. Some torture was cleaner than other torture, but a wizard didn't have to shed blood to fillet his prisoners alive, so the addition of magic made the countless sessions slightly different thant what I was accustomed to. Still, torture was torture, I kept reminding myself.

I wasn't sure if that was helping.

The hours grew into days, I think. The wizard left on occasion. Sometimes, he healed me to give my body a break, but other times, he left me bleeding.

I did not understand him. He had magic. He could do clean torture. I was already reaching my limits, three days into the ordeal. But he still chose messy forms of torture every other session.

Why?

It was not that personal, was it?

Togo.

The name kept tossing around in my head.

Whatever issue the wizard had with me was related to Togo.

They wanted to know what the mercenary had told me. But he had said nothing. And hell, even at this point, I wouldn't tell a soul what he had said, even if it meant nothing. It was the principle of the thing.

On the night of the third day — I think it was the third day, and in my previous experiences, I usually told time just fine despite that I shouldn't have been able to — the wizard reentered the tiny cell. The cell reeked of bodily fluids, and rats had started trying to crawl into the cell with me, but there must have been a magical veil keeping them just out of reach of the cell bars — the wizard was probably saving them for later.

"Who is Togo to you?" I asked. My mouth barely functioned, but I somehow got the words out.

"I'm asking the questions, Manic." The wizard snapped his fingers, causing a wave of magic to explode from his hand and enter my head. My head pounded and the blood grew hot, so hot it felt as if it were boiling within my skull and would explode at any second.

"Tell me," I hissed through the agony, voice ragged and hoarse. Despite the wizard's greatest efforts, I still hadn't screamed.

I had promised myself from a very young age that a man would never make me scream again, and it was one, if not the only promise, now, that I had kept into adulthood.

"Why?"

"Because it makes no sense to go through this trouble," I hissed. "What could he have told me to make you so worried?"

The pain stopped. Gasping in air, I let my body relax slightly in the rare reprieve of pain.

The wizard rolled up his sleeves and tied up his hair.

"He's your brother, isn't he?" I asked tightly. "Togo — you look alike, don't you? Granted, he must've gotten the good looks and good morals from the family, but —"

The wizard slapped me.

"So I am right." I grinned.

"He was my bloodkin, but he chose a different path, and I would not use good morals to describe his path," the man said harshly.

"What's your name?" I asked.

"Are you incapable of listening?" he snarled. "It is a genuine wonder how Togo put up with you for all of those months!"

All of those months.

Months of travel, of violence, of fear, of uncertainty, of risky travels, of long nights, of hearty meals, of laughs, of stories, of tears...

Months of growing together as a family. More than friends, more than allies, and more than partners.

Togo and Maude were my family — and Togo must have learned that, along the way, too, if he had fought alongside us in the end.

So, if he had betrayed the Order, he must know weaknesses, or information, or something that his brother wanted to know. But I knew nothing, really.

Was there more to it? Was this brother questioning me only to try and break my spirit, perhaps out of hatred or jealousy *because* of how close I had been to his brother?

I didn't understand that — but this wizard was making these sessions far too personal, and while he could be, no, he was insane, he was still making things too irrational. He had motives that drove him that were even darker than hatred. What drove the wizard to torture me was love for his brother, I decided. Somehow. Some twisted type of love. But love, nonetheless.

The wizard finally broke the silence, stepping backward and running a hand through his hair. "He was supposed to betray you both. Yet, he did not."

"And that angers you," I said, "because he betrayed you in turn?"

The wizard's eyes narrowed dangerously in the dim light of the lantern hanging on the wall. "Togo did not join the Order. But he joined you. So I must know what you know of him, and then you can join our ranks as the god you are."

"I've already told another of your kind that I have no interest in being a so-called god, or joining your high ranks," I said.

"Then the session shall continue."

"It is a waste of time, but have your fun."

"Every man speaks. Every man breaks. In time."

"But not the Manic," I said softly.

The wizard's eyes flickered.

I laughed. The cold sound echoed in the musty cell. "Then you do know the legend. Well, it is true. No man has broken the Manic. Three days? A week? A month? More? No amount of torture has broken me down and given my enemies a single word of what they seek. By all means, continue. But I have never been coerced into any ranks, and plenty have tried. The Order shall be no different — you, too, shall fail. And I will gladly live the rest of my long, handsome life in this cell, tortured daily, before I succumb to any man."

The wizard did not strike me, nor send any magic to invade my bones. Instead, he said softly, "Very well. It is true no man can break you. And it is true I have tried my best. Your mangled body shows this, but your strong mind reveals the truth." He smiled, his teeth glinting in the light. "If we cannot have you, Manic... Then we must execute you."

FOUR

I WOULD BE BEHEADED the next morning, in the cold, barren streets of Norkid, in the townsquare for all to see the end of the Manic.

The chains were removed, and I paced my cell in silence and in prayer.

It was funny. I had faced death many times before.

As a child, wearing rags in the streets and alleys of Norkid, I had feared death. I had cried when the men came from the shadows, used my body, and left me in the heaps of trash outside of taverns or inns. I had cried, not only from the pain inflicted upon me, but because I had truly thought, each time, that I would die, and I did not know where I would go when I died.

As a young man, I still had not known where my soul would go if I died, but by then, I had not cared. I started taking work, and jobs, and gradually became a different person. I became the Manic.

And as the Manic, as a strong, skilled mercenary, a berserker that was feared by all, I had feared nothing, not even death.

But I still had not known where I would go when I did die. Though the fact had been buried deep down, instead of haunting me like it had many broken men.

And then I had found the Light, stumbled upon the reality of Creator, and had clung onto the truth with every fiber of my being, and I had never feared death again. But I had never, of course, had anything to lose, throughout my entire life, except my life. I think this was why I had become the Manic. I had nothing, was nothing, knew nothing, and when a soul becomes oblivion itself, oblivion laughs, and uses the vessel to do its will.

But the oblivion had no right to me anymore.

And while I did not fear death, I cannot say I wanted to die. Or that I faced my execution as a genuine martyr ought to.

A true martyr would dance, sing, laugh, and rejoice in their death, because the Letters spoke highly of any soul that should die for the Light.

I was not rejoicing.

As I paced my filthy, tiny cell, the floor stained with my blood, the rats still squeaking in the stone corridor just out of reach by some magical veil, I prayed.

I prayed for peace. Supernatural peace. The peace the letters spoke of. It was supposed to transcend martyrdom, wasn't it? It was supposed to make death divine — a soul without fear or pain, embracing the afterlife and open arms of Creator.

The divine peace I asked for did not come.

The more I prayed, the more memories flooded me.

I remembered Iggy, the street urchin that hated being touched and spoke harsh words, but had hugged us so desperately before we had teleported into battle. Would he have the future he deserved? Would he find Creator?

I prayed fervently for his young soul — and I wished that I could see him once more. I had so much to tell him. I wanted to help him, too.

But it was too late.

I remembered Balder. Was he truly dead? I couldn't stand the thought — he had been young. Of course, I was not much older, but his spirit was youthful and zealous. He had been meant to lead armies, to save his people, to bring honor to his family name once more... And he had been killed defending a foreign village, alone from any friends, family, or comrades.

I had failed him.

I continued my pacing, breathing ragged.

I remembered Maude, telling stories to the sailors aboard *Sinner*, and how she had laughed and added dramatic flares to whatever ludicrous, original tale she had made. And then she had been somber and passionate while telling the stories of the Letters, too. It had not mattered the type of story, the Gifted poet had woven words together to take us all away from whatever trials that had ailed us.

Did she know how beautiful her soul was? Did she see how loved she was, by so many that met or knew her? Did she see her Gift of words as a blessing, or did she see it as worthless? Did she see her Gift of prophecy as a true form of worship and servanthood, or only as a curse?

Who would tell her these things? I could not — I would not see her again.

Why had I not said more?

I pulled at my hair, sobbing softly.

Why had I not told her so much more? Who would be there for her now? Would she be alone? Or would the Gifted alliance accept her, and love her, and give her a future — a great future she so deserved?

I remembered Togo. He had supposedly gone along with us to later betray us to the Order — but in the end, he had fought along my side, not the enemy's. Did that not mean something? And if he truly was my enemy, then the wizard — Togo's brother — would not have been so harsh with me, would he have been?

I remembered Togo's constant silence, his frustration at Maude and my shenanigans. But he had never wronged us.

He had fought alongside us. He had respected Maude's strength, and had tried to even comfort her during her darkest moments.

And he had known about me being the Manic all along, and while he had challenged my faith, he had not berated me or harmed me.

Had I shown him the love of Creator enough? Had I been a good example of the Light? Hardly, a voice inside screamed. I was a terrible example. I should have had more patience. More understanding. More kindness. And what of the end — I killed men. But then again, did Togo not tell me, when I faltered to kill the young wizard, to fight or leave? And I continued the fight — did that action earn any understanding from Togo? Did he see my determination to protect the innocent, or had he only seen hypocritical bloodshed?

Had I shown him that no matter how broken I might be, that I still knew Creator loved me, and that Creator loved him, too?

I dropped to my knees, hot tears running down my bashed and bruised cheeks and clinging to my dirty beard.

I failed Togo, too. I failed Maude, Balder, Iggy, the village, everyone.

Why? Had I not done what Creator commanded? Then why had everything fallen apart? Why was I in the enemy's clutches if I had followed the Light?

I wept, and I prayed, but no peace came over my soul, and I thought of all of the many things I wished I could have told my family.

Perhaps, if Creator were merciful, I could see them all again, in the afterlife. I could only pray so.

SIX

Dawn crept over Norkid, the sun kissing the blanket of snow that covered the distant mountains. It was my last sunrise, and I think it was the most beautiful. Streaks of pink and purple danced across the pale sky, and the cold wind billowed over the city.

People wove in and out of the streets, the men and women wearing shaggy clothes and fine clothes, the richest and poorest souls of the entire city coming out of the woodworks to see my death: the death of the Manic, the death of the killer, the death of the traitor.

I didn't care if they saw me die, so long as it was as quick as the wizards promised, and so long as I saw my family in the afterlife.

I watched the people move toward the wagon I was on, and the wagon jostled to a stop in front of the large, old wooden deck where the guillotine rested. It had not been used in a long while — the city was led by thugs, and so justice and law had not been kept under the king's rule.

It would change today.

Smoke billowed from the houses along the street, and eyes peered through the curtains — even people that didn't dare step into the streets wanted to watch me die.

I couldn't understand it — had I harmed them? Had I destroyed the kingdom? No. I was not innocent, but I had done nothing to create a vendetta against myself for these people, and yet, they hated me. Yet, they lusted for my blood. It was the nature of man to desire violence. Was my being a mercenary reason enough to thirst for my blood? Or did they care of my sins — perhaps they just wanted to see someone die. And anyone would do.

I pushed the thoughts aside. I did not want to spend my final hours, or minutes, considering the duality of man.

I wanted to spend it praying, and remembering my family, and trying, so desperately, to pray their damned souls to heaven with me so I could see them once last time after I died.

A few guards hauled me off the wagon roughly. They had teleported me just outside of the gates of Norkid, and then tossed me into the waiting wagon. They kept the metal, which ceased my Gift, around my ankles and wrists, but I was able to move mostly freely. I fell into the dirt, and the guards laughed and scoffed.

The gathering crowd in the townsquare laughed and gestured. Already, a few began throwing trash and spitting at me, but I kept my head held high. They could do whatever they liked — my body was already broken, and my spirit could not be harmed by another soul ever again.

Creator, be with me, I prayed again.

Still, even feet from the guillotine, I did not feel the divine peace settle over me.

I did not want to die, but I would not allow fear or rage to engulf me. I would not fight this — why should I? There was nothing for me here.

And had I not told Creator to take me when He saw fit? If this was the time, who was I to fight it? I had tried without ceasing to obey His will, and if this was also His will, I would follow it, even if I feared it.

I had no other choice.

I could find Maude, if she's alive, and Balder.

But they're dead.

I could find Iggy and save him.

But he would be better off with a better mentor. A family. I cannot provide that.

I could find Togo and join him — we could save many...

But he had no interest in being my partner.

The guards dragged me to the wooden platform. My legs shook slightly and I kept my mouth closed tightly as more debris was thrown at me, splattering over my bloody, torn clothes.

The crowds jeered. Children laughed and pointed. Rich businessmen watched with hungry eyes. They gathered all around the platform, yelling as the guards hauled me onto the wooden platform quickly.

Is this the end, Creator?

Should I fight? Flee?

Was I being a coward?

Was I giving in?

Should I fight — but what if this was my time, and I needed to accept things being over? For good?

Death was nothing to fear. Death was nothing evil — was it?

So why was I afraid?

Why did emptiness hollow my bones and spirit and twist my gut and rage in my soul? It felt as if the oblivion had returned for me.

I am Creator's, I said to myself, to the oblivion, over and over again.

I may fear being alone, but I do not fear death.

I said it over and over.

I will not fear anything.

But I am forsaken. Creator, why has it come to this? I know I have committed atrocities, but You cleansed me. Must I still pay in blood? Must I still deserve, earn, and accept death, despite my faith?

The four guards took me to the guillotine. It was old, creaky, and the metal blade was rusted. It would be a slow death, then.

Smoke drifted over the building tops. People filled every crevice of the square, some fighting to get closer to the platform. I watched them all and prayed: I prayed for them, and though I did not know what specifics to pray, I said softly, "Be with them, Creator. Reveal Yourself to them so that they never meet this same fate."

One of the guards heard me, because he snarled, "I would pray for a miracle, if I were you. Why don't you pray for your God to come save you?"

The other guards laughed at that, and I said nothing in return, still praying over the sea of people before me as the men held me.

The king arrived half an hour later. I stood the entire time in silence, shivering from the cold, my body mostly bare for all to see my scars, while the people grew rowdier and angrier. The morning settled heavily and the cold dug into my bones.

At the king's arrival in his fancy, beautiful carriage, the crowd erupted in cheers. Well-dressed guards guided the king to the platform slowly, and the civilians knelt and bowed before him as he moved to the platform. His cloak draped in the filth of the ground, but he waved jovially at the men, women, and children, soaking up every bit of attention.

He was tall, like Balder, but where Balder had been lean, the king was fat from corruption and greed. His short black-and-gray hair was smooth under his polished crown. He walked stiffly, and I wondered what had changed — he had not gone to war in decades. Perhaps he had tripped and fallen while standing from his bed to retrieve more wine.

I stifled a weak laugh at the thought. One of the guards nudged me hard to make me go still again.

Finally, the king reached the platform, and his security guards helped him up the steep wooden steps. He stood before the crowd and they bowed for a long moment. Then, he waved, calling, "Let's begin!"

The horde of people erupted with cheers and yells. A good portion began the chant, "Kill the Manic! Kill the Manic!"

The sound, so fiery, so passionate, so full of longing, sent a shiver down my spine.

I had not harmed innocent lives — so how could the entire city wish me dead so fervently? How had I deserved this?

I didn't.

I did nothing to deserve to be put to death — I committed sins, I killed, I stole, but I made all right, and I was not evil. But the king was evil, and even so, the kingdom served him.

It was the wickedness that Balder had seen and had been so helpless against.

And now? Balder would never restore this beautiful kingdom. It was sick, twisted, disgusting. It was a shell of its honored days of past, and now, was only a reeking cesspool of evil men and terrible acts.

Balder had died protecting another village — and had it been in vain? Was the village even still alive?

Would Norkid ever be restored? Or had I taken Balder from the kingdom's last fate?

The king waited a minute and then silenced the crowd. "On this fine winter morning, we shall put to death the Manic!"

The crowd exploded again. Waiting another minute, the king finally spoke again. "The Manic's crimes include, but are not limited to," the bastard didn't even want to take the time to make this a genuine trial, though of course, they had no evidence or justice system at work here anyway, so of course he wouldn't be bothered to list my supposed crimes in depth, "Murder, assault, disrupting the peace," what peace? "Thievery, and more."

I had done nothing to any innocent person — but I held my tongue. The crowd yelled for my blood, and there would be no stopping them now.

Even if I escaped, I would have to harm another to do so — there were too many guards on the premises, and of course, civilians would probably get in the way. Would that be worth it? I wasn't sure. I doubted it.

And so, I watched the kingdom where I had raised myself in the streets, where I had met death countless times, where I had bled in, where I had killed in, where I had grown so cold in, begging for my death, even though I did not deserve it.

The king laughed softly as the people chanted, "Kill the Manic!"

"The end of the mercenary's reign of terror ends now!" the king called.

I had left the kingdom behind years ago to begin my new life as a priest — my reign of terror had ceased long before the king decided to gain glory.

The guards pushed me to my knees.

My heart climbed into my throat.

Creator, are You with me? My heart twisted while sweat poured down my temples.

Chuckling, the guards slid my head into the guillotine. The blade hung above. The wood I was now trapped in was stained red.

The king rallied the crowds — what was he saying now? I hardly heard him. He was no doubt berating me, filling the cold, crisp morning with lies about me, and the horde would gobble it up.

Maude and Balder were gone — would they be in the afterlife? The idea of being able to embrace them both made tears burn my eyes.

But who would remember me here?

Would Iggy remember me? Would he ever think of my kindness?

Would Togo remember me? Would he find the Light eventually? Had I played a slight part in that hope?

The king stopped talking for a moment, and the guards jeered at me: "Call your God! Show us His power! Escape from here!"

I clamped my jaw shut tightly, and a few of the men at the edge of the platform spat at me.

Creator, please, let my legacy be Your love. Let my journey as a priest have done some good. Any good. Something. Please. I do not want to meet You in a minute to have You tell me that my greatest efforts amounted to nothing.

My hot tears ran down my face.

The guards rumbled with laughter. "He weeps! He knows his God cannot save him now!"

I lifted my eyes as much as I could, my neck still in the crook of the machine.

Perhaps it had been for nothing, and my life as a follower of Creator had done no good change.

But I loved the Light, and that had been enough.

The king gave a grand wave of his hand. "Kill the Manic!" he shouted.

In that moment, I kept my eyes to the heavens, but I still saw things in the corner of my eyes: I saw the king step to the side, I saw the wizard that had tortured me for days come onto the platform to stand with the king himself.

I met his gaze, then, and held it. Glee glinted in his dark eyes. It was strange to see so much evil in a soul that was supposed to be human. He might be Togo's brother, but Togo, no matter how cold or mercenary-like he was, he was human.

I looked back to the sky.

The executioner stepped forward, dressed in black, his face covered with the heavy black mask the executioners wore to hide their sacred identity — this practice was one of the wizard's rituals that the king must have adopted for today's event.

The idea of being killed by a wizard made my stomach churn.

Forcing a breath, I took in the sky above: it was mostly white now, full of dense clouds. It would snow later.

It would be a beautiful snow. Thick and fluffy. It would silence the world, and coat the Bour Mountains. It would muffle the sounds of the animals wandering in the forest. It would be beautiful — otherworldly.

I would see it, I decided, from heaven.

The executioner stepped forward, and cut the rope to the guillotine.

PART V

ONE

A FLASH OF LIGHT flooded my vision, and my body jumbled up, as if shattering in a million pieces.

I didn't have time for any final thoughts.

And then, I was gone.

Warmth covered my body.

Gentle hands held my face.

A voice, soft and kind, whispered nearby, "It's all right now. Rest. We'll take good care of you."

The angel sounded much like Maude.

I tried to open my eyes, but I couldn't. A comforting darkness took me.

"WAKE UP," A FIRM voice said. "You need to eat something."

My body felt like lead. Was heaven usually so painful?

Eyelids heavy, I managed to open one eye.

Togo sat on a chair near my bed. Thick blankets covered me, and a small fire glowed in the hearth across the tiny room. Herbs, plants, shelves of books, paintings, everything known to man covered every inch of the wall surrounding us. The sweet aroma of soup filled my nostrils.

I opened both eyes. "Togo?" I tried to speak, but my voice cracked. My throat burned, and I couldn't say more.

"Drink the soup and this medicine. It should help." Togo hesitated. "Is it all right if I feed you, or would you prefer I wake Maude to?"

"Maude..." I choked.

Togo's eyes narrowed, and he looked down at the bowl of soup in his hands. "Maude is alive. As is Balder. He teleported us from the guillotine. And Iggy is safe and sound. But that is all you must know for now. Eat, and rest."

Lifting my head off the pillow, I grabbed Togo's wrist weakly. "They're all right?"

"Yes." He sat the bowl on the tiny table beside the bed. "I'll wake Maude to feed you —"

"No," I croaked. "L-let her sleep."

Togo hesitated again, his eyebrows furrowing. "Aye." He sat back down. "She has not slept very much during the two months you were gone."

Settling back into the pillow, my insides plummeted. I still had not fully grasped the fact that I was alive, awake, and not dead. But there was more to it. "Two..."

"You were gone for two months," Togo said calmly.

I had been in the Order's grasp for two months? I had been tortured nonstop for two months?

It did not seem right — but I looked over and saw the heaviness behind Togo's eyes, and how his hair had grown slightly, past its usual short cut, and I figured it was true. Still, the reality didn't settle in, though I ignored it for now.

Togo fed me carefully. I was too weak to sit up, and couldn't move my arms much. He explained that my injuries had mostly been healed by one of the Buacach Gifted healers, but I still needed plenty of rest, and some of the scars would remain.

I said nothing in response.

The fire crackled and played in the hearth. The warm light cast shadows into the cozy room. I asked, "Where am I now?"

"A Buacach farm home," Togo said. "The farmer welcomed us in."

I had millions of questions, but the soup was making me sleepy. I leaned back and shakily pulled the blanket up over myself again.

Togo set the soup aside, and went to blow out the lantern on the table. He stopped inches from the glowing lantern. "Bjorn?"

"Yes?" I asked, voice still hoarse.

"I am sorry."

"So am I."

Togo blew out the lantern.

"Togo?" I asked.

"Yes?"

"Could you stay in the room while I sleep?"

"Yes."

I licked my chapped lips. "If I say anything while I sleep..."

"I won't listen." Togo sat in the chair again, leaning back and crossing his arms.

"You have heard me before in my sleep?" I asked, voice hoarse. I wasn't sure why I asked such a thing. But I did.

"Aye."

"Did I give myself away?"

"No." Togo looked over, head tilting. "You had nightmares like a child might. You had nightmares like I do." And then he sat as a sentry, and before long, I fell asleep again.

"He's asleep," the angelic voice said.

"He's moving," a man's voice argued. "He's awake."

I forced my eyes open. Pale morning light pierced the opened curtains beyond the two faces peering down at me.

I jerked upright, smashing my forehead into Balder's, but it didn't deter me. "Maude!" I cried, wrapping my arms around her quickly. "You're all right!" I wept, holding her tightly, and she held me back. I didn't release her but put my right arm around Balder then. "Balder! You bastard! I thought you were gone!"

Balder gave me a one-armed hug, scoffing. "Hard to kill me," he said. "But many have tried."

I slowly let them both go. "You're both well?"

Maude smiled through her tears and nodded. "Aye. The village is safe, too — you all did it... They're all right, and the Buacach Gifted Association has joined forces..." She glanced down, her face reddening. "They let me join, too. It's just as you said, Bjorn."

I grinned, but the sudden movement and exertion kicked in, and I sank back into the pillows. Maude tucked me in gently. "Rest," she said firmly. "I'm sorry we woke you. We were just so excited —"

"Thank you," I murmured.

"It's just as you said, Bjorn."

So Creator had not forsaken us, after all. I had been so sure that the darkness had won... And yet, the Light had prevailed. I had just been too lost in the dark to see it, but it had not made it less real.

And then I passed out again.

TWO

THE SAVORY AROMA OF bacon and eggs wafted through the cabin. I was out of bed by day three, and on that fine morning, beckoned by the smell of Maude cooking breakfast, I limped my way into the kitchen and dining room.

The cabin was big enough to house Maude, Togo, myself, Balder, and the man sponsoring us, a Gifted farmer by the name of Egil. Every inch of the walls were covered with decor or supplies. There was a small hearth in my room, and then a large earth in the main room, which heated the rest of the rooms. A small cat plodded along the bear rug before the giant hearth. I sat at the table, smiling tiredly.

"Eat up." Maude beamed. She set a heaping plate of breakfast on the table and I thanked her.

Egil and Balder came inside the cabin then. Their faces were rosy red, and they clomped their boots inside the foyer. "I think, dare I say it, the snow is going to melt soon," Egil declared. "I think this long winter is headed out." They hung up their coats and Maude dipped them plates of food.

Togo came out of a bedroom, pulling on his black cloak. I watched him before glancing at Maude.

Maude smiled softly at me. "It'll be nice to have spring in Buacach," she said. "Gyda has been telling me of springs here — there is much harvest, and the Red Forest is especially stunning. I have yet to explore much, though." She continued, speaking openly, "My illness is still difficult, but there have been some remedies that help some. I've been so busy learning more of the Letters and of the association I haven't had much time to explore. Well, and, of course, worrying over you." She gave me a look. It was easier to tease about my absence than speak heavily of it.

One day, perhaps, we would talk about what had happened in those two months in more depth.

But I was not ready for it now, and Maude respected it.

"Perhaps we could explore together," I agreed, digging into my breakfast.

Togo slipped out the front door without a word. Egil and Balder didn't notice, and they sat with their food, digging in and chatting heartily.

Maude met my gaze. Worry etched her freckled, pale face.

"You should eat," I said softly.

We ate, and when we finished, I stood stiffly and pulled a cloak on. Balder sighed and poured himself more coffee. "You shouldn't push yourself, Priest," he warned.

"I'm fine." *Priest. It had a nicer ring to it than Manic. Not to be vain, of course, Creator. But I'll never stop being grateful to hear such a sound as that name after... after all of this.* I started toward the door. Maude followed me, resting a protective hand on my forearm.

We stepped into the cool morning. Snow still clung to the ground of the small farmyard. A few cows munched on hay at the edge of the pasture. The farm was just outside of the Buacach kingdom, and it was a stunning area. Perfect to rest and heal up at.

But for Togo, it was like being cooped up in a prison, no doubt.

Maude and I slowly made it past the old barn. My breath came in pathetic rasps, but I didn't take a break yet. Maude helped me along.

Togo sat at the tiny creek's edge, on a big rock overlooking the white forest. Bits of snow fell around us from the tall, thick pine trees. Togo sat with his katanas in his hands, one hand resting on his knee, his hood dropped so his unkempt black hair and sharp features showed.

Maude and I stopped and sat on the rock on either side of him.

Maude said, "It's cold. You should put your hood up."

I said, "You missed breakfast. Maude's cooking is finer than ever."

But Togo said nothing in response to our slight naggings. He only watched the forest as if expecting something.

I understood. I felt as he did.

But did Maude?

I looked past him, searching her face.

Maude smiled and hugged her knees. "As it turns out, I took a brief mentorship while you were gone, Bjorn. So the training you spoke of... I have now. It is vastly different from other Gifted's training. But it means I am free to roam... as a member of their group, but a free woman, nonetheless."

Her words stood in the frigid air for a long time.

At last, Togo said, in almost a whisper, "Neither of you owe me a thing. I was hired to do a job that I did not do. So there has never been any debts." He lowered his gaze. "My days of being a mercenary are over. I only want to help others. But... I still do not believe in your God. So you... should not join me."

Maude laughed. The musical sound made me laugh, too. And we laughed, and laughed, and Togo looked between us, but the confusion in his hard eyes snapped. He laughed, too. His features lit up, and he looked almost childish, laughing between us, his shoulders bouncing.

We laughed until breathless, and then fell silent again with the dense, white forest.

After a while, I took a slow breath, exhaling and making a white puff. "When do we leave?"

THREE

Our mares snorted and stomped in the snow, restless to begin the journey. We stood out front of the cabin with our horses, fresh from the market, tacked and ready to begin our trek.

Where were we going? We didn't know.

Maude hugged Balder and Egil goodbye, and then mounted her mare. I shook their hands. "Thank you for everything," I said.

"You saved me first," Balder said cheekily. "Now, wherever Creator leads you, try to come back for a visit, aye?"

"When you return to Norkid, we shall be at your side," I said solemnly.

Balder slapped my shoulder, his boyish smile vanished, replaced by sober understanding. "In due time."

Egil gave us more food for the road. "Visit any time!" he cried jovially. "It's been a pleasure!" He stepped back, and I mounted my horse, too.

Togo shook the men's hands and mounted with a mere, "Thank you." I thought it was progress, at least.

After a delayed goodbye, we finally started on our way through the dense pine forest. The horses' breaths and our own created a chorus of white clouds in the air.

We headed south.

We didn't speak much.

We didn't plan.

We did not know where we were headed. Somewhere along the way, Creator would show us where to be, and we would be there, and another story would begin and end.

We rode through the white snow, with our crimson pasts far behind us.

Author's Note

I wrote this novel while I was running.

Running from diagnoses.

It was silly. One cannot run from their own broken body. But my mind tried fleeing from accepting the fact that I was "sick" and "broken."

I ran for about a year, and during that year, I took a few months... and wrote this.

Bjorn taught me to love the life I have. Maude taught me that kindness to others is still worthwhile. Togo taught me that strength doesn't look how I always want it to.

And ultimately... This book taught me to stand strong and brave in the truth, even if the world stands against me.

See, my mom was chronically ill for most of my childhood and into my adulthood, and I was her caregiver for years. I remember her crying when people would tell her,

"If you had more faith, you would be healed." It was not true. And I grew angry at the world for speaking such lies to her. Finally, when I got sick, I heard the same voices, on social media, in church, etc... Even now, as I am treating, and slowly, getting better, I mourn seeing so many people wrongly belittle the suffering in the name of the Light.

But it took this novel to teach me what faith truly is, I think, though obviously, thousands of books could be written on the topic, and barely scratch the surface. But this is my drop of water in the ocean. And I have some people to thank for making this drop of water possible.

My parents, for their nonstop support, and their insistence that I get treatment, even when I was afraid. Thank you guys for supporting me and helping me survive.

My brother, Kody, for building us a house to live in, for helping me on the days I can barely function, and for brightening my rough days. Thank you for being my best friend.

My friend, Irene, for being there when I was nothing but a depressed blob crying over dumb things. Thanks for reminding me of the Light and pushing me to keep fighting.

My doctors. I don't want to list names, but you all deserve a shoutout, at least. Thank you for saving me and pushing me forward.

My readers. I wasn't sure how this novel would do — and you all made the launch so worthwhile. I was scared to show so much of my heart Thank you for reading, and being here. Here's to many more books to come.

My backers. Effie Joe, Blue Ink Books, Ling, Colleen, Dawn, Josefine, Kylie, Craig, Kenyon, Becca, Ashton, Meredith, Cortney, Kristin, Sirrah, Cherelle, Althea, John, Bonita, Teddi, Troy, Abby, Michaela, Mickey, Lyle, Kass, R.J., Naticia, William, Carly, Jason, Ollie, Daniel, Yakira, Justin, Marlene, Jason, Hannah, KLG, Erudessa, Eva, Ken, Laura, Laurel, Kody, Kim, Wyngarde, Will It Work, Julie, Michael, Nicolas, Justin, McKenna, Dona, Dead Fish Books.

THANK YOU

Thank you so much for reading AMONG THE CRIMSON SNOW. If you enjoyed the novel, I would so appreciate a review on your favorite online retailer. Reviews help authors a ton, and a simple review can go a long way. They also help me push on on hard days!

Music Playlist

I Am A Stone, Demon Hunter

Hello My Old Heart, The Oh Hellos

Rule #13 Waterfall, Fish In A Birdcage

Wayfaring Stranger, Poor Man's Poison

Hollow, Fenris

Blood Upon the Snow, Bear McCreary &
Hozier

Don't Go, Christopher Dennis Coleman

Find Me, Aviators

Also By

THE INFIDEL BOOKS

Paradise Lost, The Infidel Books #0

The Divided Nation, The Infidel Books #1

The Grim Alliance, The Infidel Books #2

The Mercenary's Deception, The Infidel Books #3

The Blood Republic, The Infidel Books #4

Emmanuel, an Infidel Books short story prequel

Lockdown, an Infidel Books short story prequel

Hunted, an Infidel Books novelette prequel

GLORY EPOCH BOOKS

Up From the Ashes, Glory Epoch Books #1

To The Grave, Glory Epoch Books #2

ROGUE SURVIVORS

War of the Fallen, Rogue Survivors #1

Icarus is Burning, Rogue Survivors #2

Of Fallen Gods, Rogue Survivors #3

REMNANT TRILOGY

Golgotha

Tabor

Aceldama

STAND ALONES

A Solstice of Fire and Light

Seek

War: A Collection of Poetry and Free Verse
Among the Crimson Snow

CHILDREN'S FICTION

Winter of the Bees
Leon Gains and the Expedition to the Void, The Legacy Books #1
Leon Gains and the Serpent's Curse, The Legacy Books #2
Leon Gains and the End of the Realms, The Legacy Books #3
Freedom (coming soon)
Stan the Snail Finds His Purpose
Mo Finds His Way Home

ANTHOLOGIES

Where Giants Fall
Run From The Dead
The Depths We'll Go To

ANGELA R. WATTS

LIFE

Ganbatte!

Perchance to Dream

Don't Go In The Water

Tales from the Forest

Nerdology

Streets of Ash and Fire

Laser Cannons and First Contact

COLLABORATIONS

DARK with Dawn E. Dagger

DEATH BARGAIN (Late Hours Saga #1) with Irene Sylvan

AUTHOR BIO

ANGELA R. WATTS is the bestselling and award-nominated author of The Infidel Books and the Remnant Trilogy. She's been writing stories since she was little, and has over 40 works in print, ranging from gritty adult novels to clean children's fiction. Angela is a Christian, editor, article writer for magazines and publishers, founder of Speculative Fiction Society and WRITEGIG, and artist. If she's not working, she's outside looking for bugs or snakes. She lives in Tennessee with her family and many pets. You can get in touch with Angela and follow the journey on social media.

Website and newsletter: angelarwatts.com
Instagram: @angelarwattsauthor
Facebook: https://www.facebook.com/AngelaRWattsauthor

Made in the USA
Columbia, SC
04 November 2024